PAGES BURNED

PAGES BURNED

Tanner Taylor

Tanner Taylor
2015

First Printing: 2015

ISBN: 978-0692421437

An all too familiar storm was brewing that night in the small town of Eden Isle, Louisiana. A maelstrom of anger, sadness, confusion, and hatred boiled in the depths of Hayley's heart. Another family dinner eaten in silence. The small clinks of forks and knives provided the only reprieve. A family sitting at the table in a tension filled room. Once again forced to escape to her room to avoid the whirlwind of shouts and verbal violence, Hayley poured out her emotions into poetry while fruitlessly attempting to drown out the fights with loud music. The stories she wrote of a different life – one free from the tears and heartache – failed once again to shift her mood. Sleep became the only thing routine and pleasant in this crumbling home.

Her control on the world around her had long since been torn from her own hands. The constant battling between her mother and father tore at her mind and heart every second of every day. Her room had become nothing more than a sanctuary from the world outside of her door and window. The nights at home grew more and more unbearable for Hayley and her sister, Caroline. The two daughters of Amy and Eli Audige were forced to watch their family being torn apart a little more each day.

Home life should not be this hard. The girls were used to their parents' jobs getting in the way at times. Amy was a sales manager for a local manufacturer and Eli was a realtor in New Orleans. Amy's odd hours and travel mixed with Eli's commuting and late nights at the office made for more than a few nights that the family was missing a piece or two. This was nothing too out of place for a family with two parents with full time careers. Her family was accustomed to a comfortable lifestyle, nothing extraordinary compared to the rest of the town. Her family fit right in with the fold of the population. However, something in the gears of her family went awry and now the entire machine was falling apart. Small tiffs normal for any couple had evolved into shouting matches and slamming doors. A couple could only fight so much before the rift between them became too great to cross again. The threat of divorce was no surprise to Hayley, but the knowledge of its possibility did not lighten the burden at all. A night of dry eyes was something that she had not known for quite some time.

Dealing with classmates was no easy task for Hayley either. Being eighteen and in her last year of high school, she had gotten used to being bullied regularly for being "different" ever since she was in middle school. Her slender frame and fair skinned complexion were not out of place in her school. Her personal style, however, could not have been more discordant with the other students. Her auburn hair was accented by bright red-orange highlights rising from the ends like flames from a torch. Her clothing tended toward the alternative artsy style. Her torn jeans, self-altered shirts, eclectic scarves and jewelry drew mystified looks from students and some teachers alike. She was a very introverted girl, preferring the company of her books and sketchpads to that of her classmates, not that many would have offered it in the first place. The disapproval of her alternate style was even more pronounced because her sixteen-year-old sister was a very typical teenage girl in both personality and style. Caroline fit in perfectly with her trendy clothes, straight blonde hair, and care free demeanor. In a school full of doctors' and lawyers' children all striving to become doctors and lawyers themselves, Hayley stuck out like a peacock in a world full of doves. Yet no matter how much she stuck out in a crowd, her voice was still lost in the echo.

School work had never been a problem for either of the Audige sisters. While Caroline excelled in science and math, Hayley was a standout in English and creative writing. She often spilled the emotions from her heart about the ongoing issues at home into her poetry and stories. She kept her struggles laced up in metaphors so that no one outside would have knowledge of her crumbling world. Her poetry won her acclaim amongst those in the English department and teachers often would tell her of the great potential they saw in her. Unfortunately, every time someone would lift her up at school, someone else would be there to knock her down again. Caroline would come to her defense against the other students whenever she could, but as an underclassman, she could not be with her sister at all times.

The sisters lounged around the fire pit behind the house late that night as they usually had many nights before. The water of the canals sat still just beyond their small backyard. The soothing sounds of the small wakes and waves rhythmically colliding with the canal walls made for a peaceful ambiance to the warm fires. Stark shadows were cast across the stone tile patio surrounding the fire pit. The lights of the golf club could be seen in the distance. It was always a comforting thing for each of them, no matter what was going on in their lives. The amber-orange glow warmly lit the backside of the white house and gave birth to large shadows from the furniture and landscaping that lined the concrete patio. The stone lined fire pit warmed the girls' bare feet as the temperature dipped down into the 50's for the first time in weeks.

Caroline sipped her tea as she worked on her homework in the dim light of the fire. Hayley scribbled down more poems and doodles in her tattered old notebook. The emerald cover was littered with scratches, creases, and worn drawings. The binding of the notebook had all but disintegrated away from the constant wear and tear of use and stowing in her backpack. The more she wrote the more frustrated and emotional she became. Poems that did not meet her standards were torn from the notebook. Hayley tossed the rejected works into the fire. As the flames engulfed the pages, Hayley would lift both hands like a wizard as though she was causing them to burn. She watched the ashes and embers rise out of the flames wishing they would reappear as phoenixes and carry her away from the hell in which she was currently living. The flames were no longer only a supply of warmth for Hayley, but a symbol of hope and change.

Nothing could change Hayley's desire to throw her life into the fire and rise from the flames as something new, something stronger, something invincible. Hayley stowed her notebook in her backpack and returned back into the house. As she sulked back up the deep cherry wooden stairs and into her room for the night her mind wandered to thoughts of a return to normalcy, a return to a time before. Her room once again became her refuge from the real world.

She scanned around her room and observed all of the things she had made and collected. Poetry, sketches, paintings, and sewing supplies lined her desk and nightstand. Her collection of novels fully stocked her bookshelf providing a colorful backdrop to the otherwise neutral tones in her room. Her bed sat below a large black and white phoenix painted across her dull cream colored walls. She took on the task of painting the large black creature herself a year ago when her parents first started showing signs of discord. Above the firebird were the words "Dreams are wishes burned onto your heart." These were the words Hayley lived by throughout high school.

Her dreams guided her through these days and helped her deal with the demons she was forced to deal with every hour. The dreams of a teenage girl that saw little support from her family only fueled Hayley more to break out of her own shell. To shatter the mold she felt she was being forced into by her family's current standing.

= *2* =

The morning began as calmly as a car crash. Hayley was awoken to the sounds of shouts and slamming doors downstairs. Eli and Amy were fighting once again. Hayley refused to leave her room and venture through the warzone. She instead remained on her bed, held captive by her own pain, trying to drown out the noise by holding her pillow over her head. The swirling anger inside her mind only sped up the arrival of the tears that soon followed. Caroline, frightened out of her own room by the slamming doors, saw that Hayley's door was still closed and went in to seek shelter. Upon seeing Hayley in this emotional state, Caroline began to fruitlessly attempt to comfort her sister.

"I'm here Hay" Caroline said softly, sitting next to her sister and rubbing her back.

"I can't take this anymore!" Hayley cried, "How can anyone be expected to take this at home and then go and deal with the idiots I have to deal with at school?"

"Hayley," Caroline placed her hand on Hayley's back, "none of them know what we're going through. Almost none of them will ever understand."

"I'm so sick of everything. I hate them all, Caroline."

"Don't say that. It's only high school. Don't let things get to you, sis. The people bringing you down are not worth your time." Caroline reminded Hayley. She always had a knack for sounding wise beyond her years.

"Please don't start on this again, I know it's only high school. You don't have to take the harassing from people that I do." Hayley pleaded.

"I mean it, Hayley. These four years do not and cannot define who you are. You define who you are, not other people. You're so much stronger than you give yourself credit for. You're better than all of this petty nonsense. College will be completely different for you. You have a whole new chance to start fresh and find new real friends. Just stay calm and realize that it's only a minor speed bump. I'm only trying to give a perspective of your situation--"

"My situation?" Hayley interrupted, shooting upright and knocking Caroline's hand away. "What's that supposed to mean?"

Caroline shook her head, "Nothing, I'm just saying that things may be easier for you if you were able to ignore the people that do nothing but bring you down and make you feel awful. You know that I will always do anything you need me to do to help you."

"I know. I get what you're saying." Hayley said grudgingly.

Caroline failed to think of anything else to say and retreated from the room leaving a noticeable tension behind. This very same conversation happened more and more since their parents began fighting. Hayley knew that her sister was only trying to help her. She also knew that she was completely right. Life would be so much easier if she could just brush off the people at school like they brushed her off, like Caroline said. Caroline was always there with comforting words, although Hayley had a hard time seeing her sister's compassion at times.

As stubborn as Hayley's mind could be, Caroline's words did not go unheeded in the following weeks. Hayley began trying to brush off any sort of bullying that came her way at school. Making a conscious effort to ignore her tormentors appeared to be doing the trick. A certain fire began to ignite inside of her heart. She began feeling that maybe she could best her foes. Her mind was starting to look past what the other students would say and do. The immature names and constant hounding began having less effect on her.

As fast as her new walls were built, they came crashing down. The only boy she had ever had a crush on, Devin Broussard, for the first time was laughing with his friends while they bullied her. He laughed and encouraged with his friends as they watched the girls do the dirty work. Devin stood behind high fiving and joking with his friends, calling out names. The girls in the group constantly knocked her books out of her hands, violently shoved her against her locker, and tore up poetry and other work that fell from her notebooks. Devin had never participated in things like this before. She wondered what would cause him to completely change the way he acted toward her. *Why now? What did I do to him?* Hayley thought to herself. The name calling usually never bothered Hayley much, until today. Hearing the names come from

Devin hit Hayley like a truck. Coming home with new bruises, mental and sometimes physical, quickly took its toll on her mind.

Devin's involvement, as minor as it had been, felt like a knife to the heart. Handsome, athletic, and yet something was slightly mysterious about him. Devin seemed to be everything Hayley wanted. His group of friends appeared to be different than him. It was the kind of difference that Hayley knew was there but could not put her finger on. It seemed as though he did not fit in with his own group. His disposition was never quite the same as the others in his clique, like he did not actually want to be with them. Nearly any time he was with them, he was very quiet and would not join in much of anything they did. Instead, he would often stand off on the side and fiddle with his cell phone.

He was quite different than Hayley on the outside. His clean cut look and cool demeanor made him very popular among the girls at school. He was a two-sport athlete, playing soccer and baseball for the school. Hayley, however, felt that there was something hiding inside of him that most people did not know about. A side of him that most people had never seen before.

If anyone else had done it, Hayley would not have been nearly as hurt. Her days of tenacity at school had collapsed into insecurity once again. Later the same day after the incident at school, Hayley's phone rang and a familiar voice was on the other end.

"Hello?" Hayley answered.

"Hayley?" Devin asked. "How have you been?"

Hayley did not want to talk to him at all, but forced herself to, "What do you want? Didn't get enough of a chance to take some shots at me at school?"

"That's why I called," Devin uttered with a serious voice. "I wanted to apologize for what my friends and I did. You don't deserve that. I never should have gone along with them in doing that."

"Devin, just stop. I don't want to hear it. You don't know what it's like at all to deal with this. Nearly every day someone has to do or say something to me. Either don't join them or try to make them grow up. I thought you were better than that." Hayley hung up the phone without letting Devin respond.

Hayley could hear the sincerity in his voice, however, she did not know if he could see through her attitude. The cry for help from a girl at the end of her rope and needing someone to pull her back. Hayley felt that she selfishly attempted to make Devin feel worse for what had happened. Deep in her mind she knew that part of her did not want to actually hurt Devin's feelings, but part of her wanted to give him a taste of his own medicine. She could not allow herself to hide from her emotions anymore. It was time that she try to make things change.

She wanted to be mad at him so badly that it hurt, wanting nothing more than to be with him instead. He hurt her with the things he said. *Sticks and stones*, she thought, but it felt more like swords and sledgehammers. Her mind could not comprehend why he would join in with his friends after never taking part before. Her heart was pulling much harder than her brain when she contemplated accepting his apology. Something about his words made her believe that he was nothing like the person he appeared to be that afternoon. Devin was the only boy to ever affect her mind this much. The very thought of this terrified Hayley to no end. She was scared of the idea of Devin's attention. *What if he did like me? What if I was driving him away? What if I already had?*

Despite the constant distress Hayley felt from having to deal with mean and rude students at school, she was still able to focus enough to keep her grades higher than nearly everyone in her class. This became a much needed source of pride to her. She always loved learning new things and coming up with original stories and ideas every day. Creating allowed her the valuable opportunity to get her emotions out in a constructive manner. Each and every poem she wrote spoke the emotions of her heart and her mind that she could not express otherwise. Dealing with her parents split and her ordeals at school melted away when she picked up her pen and paper, no matter how frustrating the task of writing got at times.

The knowledge that her senior show was fast approaching allowed Hayley to focus on the things she loved even more and provided another opportunity for her to showcase her talent. This was her moment after four years. She had been part of a few small shows throughout high school, but this was her main stage at last. Long grinding days in school had become more worthwhile in the weeks leading up to the show. Being in the senior show allowed

Hayley to receive the recognition for her works that she felt she deserved. More importantly, it gave Hayley the attention she so desperately desired. The spotlight would finally be on her, if only for a few moments. All of her work would be worth the extra time and effort she put in once it was all on display for everyone to see. She found it difficult to present her work to other people outside of school. Her parents did not appear to show much interest in her poetry either. She felt that they did not truly understand the extent of what she was expressing in her work.

= 3 =

The senior shows for Theroux High School happened in mid April. The school gym had been converted into a full gallery and was lined wall to wall with the work of all of the artistic senior students. Carpeting had been laid throughout the makeshift gallery. Paintings of mountain landscapes and still life works were mixed in amongst paintings of ambiguous colors, lines, and splatters. Across the gallery from the paintings were the sculptures and ceramics. The poetry displays were located next to the many clay masks and sculptures of angels and animals. A six foot table lined with cheese, crackers, and drinks sat in the center of the gallery. Hayley parked herself at her station and waited for the crowd of visitors to come in. She was dressed in black pants and a black and white striped tank top with a red cardigan sweater over that. Her hair was styled nicely as well. Dressing up was not something Hayley liked to do. The unfamiliar styles made her uncomfortable and self-conscious.

Hayley put her poetry on display for everyone to see. Her general indifference to the show itself did not stop her from getting butterflies in her stomach. The small section allotted for poetry was often lost amongst the overload of colors and shapes of the visual art in the gallery. True interest never crossed the faces of those who stopped to actually read the poetry displayed. During the quiet set up time, rain began to fall outside. The drops pinged and crashed on the metal roof of the Theroux gymnasium. The noise created by the constant fall of the rain was relaxing to Hayley. It helped to quell her nerves about the show.

Each student finished hanging their work and prepping their tables. The doors to the gym opened and family and friends began to file into the gymnasium. Quiet conversations could be heard as the guests walked into the show. The parents greeted their children and the friends began to chat with one another. The traffic in the room flowed slowly around each and every display.

Hayley went through the motions, gave empty thank you's, and answered any and all of the questions presented to her. Like a trade show full of uninterested clients she watched person after person glance at her display and walk right past. She stood in silence for the majority of the show as the questions she was quick to answer were few and far between, her mind began to wander. *Is this over yet? Does anyone actually care about this show?* It grew increasingly difficult for Hayley to take the whole situation seriously as she watched more and more people walk through the gallery with nothing more than a glossed over empty stare.

As it went every year, it was mostly parents who came to see the artwork and poetry. Their eyes skimming from one to the next, not really paying attention to any, giving the students bits of cliché praise whether they deserved it or not. Hayley's current home life had given her a cynical outlook toward the whole event. Her excitement of creation had often been suffocated by the constant emotional rollercoaster enough that she would have rather just skipped the show all together. She waited for her parents to come and see what she had been working on all year, but they never came, no doubt being caught up in another fight.

Hayley, though upset by their lack of attention, was not surprised that this happened. It was just one more thing to go wrong in her family. Caroline, however, made sure that she was there to support her big sister. The annoyance of her absentee parents soon morphed into indifference. She couldn't stay mad at something she subconsciously expected. The school year would be done in a little over a month and Hayley would be free from this place as she headed off to Tulane in the fall. In her mind this was the only thing that was going according to plan. Her family was falling apart and her classmates had exiled her, but now she would finally get the chance to start over with new people.

"Hey hey, Hay." Caroline chuckled as she walked up to her sister's display.

Hayley shook her head and smiled at her sister. "You dork."

Caroline gave Hayley a large, goofy, over-exaggerated smile. "How goes it?"

"Same as usual for any of these shows. More or less just trying to stay awake through it all." Hayley glanced around the room, "So what happened to Mom and Dad coming tonight?"

Caroline shrugged, "They said were going to come a little after I left, but I'm sure that went south really fast. They fight so much more when they're alone."

Hayley shook her head, knowing that is exactly what happened, "Tell me about it. I'm so sick of hearing that all the time. Nothing but tension and arguing every single day. I can't deal with it anymore."

"Yeah," Caroline moved to Hayley's side to see her poetry, "just try not think about it so much and focus on your own stuff. Nothing we can do about it now."

Hayley ignored the advice of her sister before continuing on, "So what do you think?"

"These are good, Hayley. Like really good."

Hayley smiled, "Thanks, some weren't the easiest to write."

"I can tell. They aren't the easiest to read either since I know exactly what they're about." Caroline finished reading the last of the poems and looked around the room. "Well I'm going to move along now, have fun with the rest of the show."

"Alright, I'll see you at home. Thanks for coming."

"Of course." Caroline waved to her sister and walked on to the next display.

As the show came to a close, the gallery began to empty. Hayley began gathering her papers off of her table and packing them away into her burgundy canvas bag. She pulled her poems from the wall behind her, pulling the tacks and leaving them in the cup on the table, and slipped them in her folders. Once she had tucked the last folder away, she caught a glimpse of the shoes of someone standing nearby to her right. She hoped it was not anybody who wanted to read the poetry she had just put away. The bright red shoes glowed against the dark carpeting of the gallery. Hayley lifted her gaze to see Devin standing next to her station waiting for her. He was cleaned up a little more than usual tonight. His usual t-shirt and worn jeans had been replaced with a scarlet and navy blue plaid buttoned shirt and stylish dark blue jeans. His aviator sunglasses rested atop his rusty blond hair. He stood with a nervous half smile as he worked up the courage to try and make amends.

"So, how did it go tonight?" Devin asked.

"As expected." Hayley quietly replied, sliding her bag over her shoulder, "Not a whole lot of interest from anyone. What are you doing here?"

"Oh you know," Devin chuckled quietly "to appreciate the fine arts. I'm quite the connoisseur of everything from paintings to literature—"

"Are you finished?" Hayley interrupted Devin's obvious sarcasm.

"Okay, okay. I came to try to make up for the other day. I don't think that my phone call was enough to make up for the way I acted. Can I take you out to eat and hopefully explain why I acted the way I did? Nothing too serious, just two friends having some dinner. I understand if you don't want to go."

"Why? Why should I go with you?" Hayley curtly asked.

"I'm not saying you should, just hoping that you do so I can show you I'm really not who I appeared to be with my friends."

"And how would I know you aren't just putting up a front now?" Hayley understandably questioned what brought about this sudden change in him.

"I know it's hard to only trust my word, Hayley. I just hope that you can take the chance and let me prove it to you and I think you'll be surprised with what you find."

"I don't know that I even think you deserve a chance."

"I know that I don't deserve one. I do want you to know that I am sorry for how I've treated you, though" Devin began to turn to leave, disappointed that Hayley did not seem interested in his offer, "I guess I will just see you later then."

"Devin, wait," Hayley paused, tapping her hand on the table as though she was hard pressed to find her next words to say. "I probably shouldn't do this, but I will take the chance and go with you, plus, I'm really hungry." She let a little laugh slip. Hayley accepted Devin's request hoping that he could say something that would make her understand him a little more.

"Great," He said smiling, "thank you, Hayley."

"I'll be finished here in a few minutes. I just need to go and lock up my things," She slung her bag over her shoulder, "go ahead and wait for me out front."

Hayley attempted to mask her own emotions by asking so many questions. She deflected Devin's sincere apology and offer to bury the hatchet in a half-hearted attempt and hide her own nerves. Not wanting to seem too excited, Hayley hid behind this false attitude to distance herself from the situation. She was a girl of too many faces. During the days she was the mistreated book worm who took her punches without a fight, but upon arriving at home she became the depressed and scared daughter of a broken marriage. The true Hayley hid inside of her writing. The mentally strong, emotionally expressive heroine she always wrote about, the girl who would stand up to those who stood against her. The girl who could open her own eyes to the reality of her world and make the changes she needed to make to come out ahead and come out even stronger than before.

Hayley walked through the long Theroux halls and back to her locker. She stowed her bag then grabbed her purse. She closed her locker, and began to walk away. Suddenly she stopped and thought for a moment before turning back toward her locker. Upon opening the emerald metal door, she glanced into the mirror she had hung on its backside. Hayley stared into her own hazel eyes. The shade of her eyes seemed to vary from day to day, green to brown and back again. She noticed that they were a pretty shade on the green side today. An uncontainable smile began to spread across Hayley's face.

Her excitement of what just occurred was undeniable. She had been waiting for something like this to happen for the longest time. After everything that had transpired over the past few months, after things seemed to only get worse every day, something finally swung in her favor. This was her chance to find out who Devin really was. She could finally have a full conversation with him and pick his brain. Was he really the guy that he had claimed to be or was he just as two-faced as the rest of them? She fixed her hair behind her ear and made sure it was all in place before closing her locker and heading to the front of the school to meet Devin.

= *4* =

Just outside the front steps of the school, Devin was waiting in his truck. The metallic black pickup shined in the school's lights and water droplets shimmered across its body. Hayley came to its side and opened the door. "Hello again" Hayley giggled.

"Hey you, where should we go?" Devin pulled out of the drop-off circle and toward the street.

"I don't really know, I kind of figured you had something in mind," again Hayley chuckled out an excited sentence, "Do you not?"

"No I have an idea, just checking."

"Okay. Are you going to tell me?"

"Of course not," Devin laughed, "Just wait and see."

They drove out of the school lot and made their way down the road to the mystery destination. Each time a possible destination passed, Hayley's nervous anticipation grew and grew. She held off her desire to ask Devin where they were going because if she knew one thing about tonight it was that he was not going to spill the beans on his plan.

"So what made you feel like you needed to take me out tonight?" Hayley questioned.

"Like I said earlier, I just didn't feel right about what happened. Something wasn't sitting right inside me and I knew I had to try to fix that. As I said, that's not the real me."

Hayley smirked, "Well, so far you're not doing such a terrible job."

"Hopefully, I do better than just 'not terrible,'" Devin awkwardly let a bit of laughter slip with these confused words, "I think that I'll be able to explain everything a little more thoroughly once we get there."

Hayley found it harder and harder to keep up her tough façade. Her excitement of being alone with the boy that she had so longed for the chance to be with was burning away at her brain. She was struggling more now to find the attitude that she had so easily produced earlier that same night. Undoubtedly, her walls would be easy to break down once the two of them made it to their destination. Hayley hoped the same would be true for Devin. She wanted so badly to find out who was truly behind his mask.

The car continued down the rain soaked roadway. The rain had long since ceased yet the city remained with its new wet shimmer. City lights and neon signage reflected off of the freshly saturated pavement. Devin began to slow the car and turn into the parking lot behind Josiah's, a casual bistro a few blocks from the school. The fascia that covered the outside of the building provided an inviting warm red welcome to all.

The hostess greeted and sat the two of them outside on the covered patio near the ebony wrought iron fencing surrounding the restaurant. The intricately crafted fence was beginning to show its age with small patches of rust working their way through the dark metal. The outdoor tables were set under a large gold awning that protected them from the rain. Both Hayley and Devin sat in awkward silence for a few minutes, both waiting for the other to find the right words to start a conversation. Devin fidgeted with the menu while Hayley stared down the road along the side of the restaurant. To the reprieve of each of them, the waiter came and broke the silence.

"Are you two ready to order?"

"I think so," Hayley said confidently, "I'll have the crawfish étouffée."

"And I'll have the sausage po' boy," Devin closed out the order.

"Thank you, I'll get that put in right away for you," the waiter cheerily said while collecting the menus.

"Étouffée huh? Sounds fancy," Devin laughed.

"You shush," Hayley smiled and stuck her tongue out, "It's delicious." She shook her head and quickly changed the subject, "anyway, you said you would explain to me what's been going on."

"Yes, I did say that. I don't know how much you really know about me, Hayley. I know we've never really talked much at all. I'm not really exactly who I appear to be at school though."

"So you've said. You just haven't really clarified what you mean by that." She poked at the table with her fork as she awaited his answer.

"Well I, um—What I mean by it is—is that I know what you're going through. I know what it's like to be cast aside." Devin said, fiddling with the napkin in front of him.

"What do you mean you know? How could you possibly know what's going on in my life?" Hayley sternly questioned, prying for some sort of answer, "You've barely spoken to me."

"Yeah, you're absolutely right. I don't know your entire story, but I do see what happens at school and, regrettably, have been involved with it sometimes. I know what it's like to not fit in."

"How do you know? I never seen you with anyone outside of the popular group." Hayley continued to try and pull more information from Devin.

"Yeah, maybe now. I learned to swim is really what it amounts to. I found out how to fit in enough to make it bearable. Sports definitely helped give me a place in the school." He looked around the restaurant before continuing, "Before I moved here from Shreveport I was just like you. I loved being creative and drawing. I was always up near the top of the class. I loved who I was, but once I hit high school, that's when the bullying started. Kids would knock me over in the hall and destroy my sketchbooks." Devin began to get visibly frustrated as he dug up his old memories, "They would make fun of me because I used to paint sets for the plays and helped put on the actors' make up. All of this just because I was creative with my hands and always liked learning new art styles. I still to this day don't really know why they made fun of it. I hated it. I hated them, and I mean *hated*. I would hide away from everyone at school because I was so angry."

"Oh wow, Devin. I had no idea you had been through all of that." Hayley put her hand out toward him to offer support although he didn't seem to notice. She looked at her hand and awkwardly pulled it back, "I guess you really do know what it feels like."

"That's not the worst of it. As angry as I got, I could put up with them making fun of me. It was when I wasn't the target anymore that it got bad. My parents split early sophomore year and, oh man, did they have a field day with that. I was constantly stressed at school because I was always thinking about what was going on at home. When the idiots at school got word of what had happened, that's when they started making fun of my family. I had had enough."

"What happened?" Hayley quietly asked.

Devin took a deep breath, "As it is with most bullies, one piece of information spiraled out of control and into lies and exaggeration. I'm not proud of this, but this kid, Brett, just picked the wrong day to mess with me. I was already mad about the whole divorce thing and he decided that he was going to start spreading rumors about my parents. I found out that during gym class he was telling people that my dad was a drunk and beat my mom. He was saying that was why they split, which was not even remotely close or correct and-" He got quiet.

"And what?" Hayley asked.

"I just lost it. I tackled him into the bleachers and started just punching him. I had to have hit him a good five or six times before people pulled me off of him. It's kind of a blur at this point."

"Oh my God, Devin. That's awful." Hayley quietly sat shocked at what she was hearing.

"I know it is. I hate myself for letting him get to me like that. Even worse is that he ended up in the hospital that night and didn't come back to school for at least a week because he hit his head so hard on the bleachers when I tackled him. Luckily, I only got suspended for a week for it because I had never done anything close to that before. I've never done anything like that since. I've never even felt that angry either."

"Wow, so what happened when you went back?"

"I never went back. My dad pulled me out of that school when it happened. He had to pull some strings to get me in down here because of the incident. Mr. Johnstone kind of reluctantly let me in on the condition that nothing like the other incident happen again. Sort of like a one and done scenario."

"I can see why you got so angry. Did the other kid come out alright?"

"Yeah, he was kind of messed up for a couple days during the week he was gone, but he got better. Turned out the hit on the bleachers gave him a pretty nasty concussion. I made sure that I apologized to him before we moved. I haven't talked to him since I did, though. Anyway, like I was saying, I know what it's like to get tortured at school."

"Wow, I can't believe that. I've definitely been angry enough to do that sometimes. I guess that I've just been lucky enough to hold it in so far. I didn't realize that you had been through so much. I had you pegged all wrong. Sorry." Hayley sat back in her chair feeling slightly guilty for thinking she was so different from Devin.

"I don't want you to fall like I did. I wear a mask at school. That's why I haven't joined any of the arts here. I didn't want to go back into the minefield. All that it has taught me is that being fake is so much worse than being yourself. It may be easier through the day, but I hate every day because of it. I try so hard to be like them just to have peace at school." His openness came as an enormous surprise to Hayley. Devin continued his frustrated explanation, "It makes my head want to explode. I see all of the talent that this school has and the great people I'm missing out on because I'm so scared of falling again. That's why I'm going to do whatever I can to stop my friends from bothering you like they have."

The certainty with which Devin spoke drew Hayley into him more and more. She was hooked on every word he said. Hayley could not believe how close his story was to her own. She finally believed that he was actually telling the truth about it all the whole time.

"Well thank you, Devin. I really appreciate that. I've been pretty good lately with letting it bounce off me. I've had very bad days, though. There have been days when I feel that I can't take it anymore and want to find a way to end it all. I never tried to do any of that, though. I haven't tried ending anything, myself or anyone else."

With every word Hayley could feel her walls crumbling around her. The new found freedom she felt was so refreshing and empowering. She felt as though she was able to tell Devin anything and he would understand just how she was feeling.

"Keep it that way. The bad people aren't worth your emotion. I let it get the best of me. Don't do that to yourself. I can tell you're a great girl. Don't change at all." He quietly said and smiled.

"I haven't told anyone at school about this, but my parents are also going through a divorce right now too. I hate every second of it."

"Oh no, I'm so sorry to hear that Hayley, that's such a rough time. I'll be sure to never mention it to anyone," Devin held his hand out to Hayley and she placed her own hand on top of his and a whirlwind of excitement exploded in her heart.

"Thanks. I just don't even know what to do anymore." She said.

"Well, I'm always around if you need someone to talk to. I know we've only hung out tonight but I think I might be able to at least help a little."

"Thank you," Hayley accepted with a shy smile.

As the couple continued to talk through their meal, sharing stories of family and mutual experiences, they realized their quick dinner had turned into a few hours and the late evening turned to late night.

"Oh yikes, I better get you home, huh?" Devin blurted out after checking his watch.

"Yeah I guess so, don't worry about the time. It will be fine. It's not like it's four in the morning. My parents don't really worry about me getting into much trouble."

Hayley reached for the check but Devin stopped her hand. "I'll take care of that." Devin said with a smile.

"Are you sure?"

"Definitely. It's the least I can do."

"Well thanks, Devin."

The couple made their way back to Devin's truck, walking shoulder to shoulder. Devin started the engine and pulled out of the lot. He appeared, to Hayley, to be driving slower than he had previously done on the way to the restaurant. Hayley could find no reason to hurry this night along by mentioning it.

"If you don't mind me asking, why did your parents split up?" Hayley questioned, the thought had been nagging her since he first mentioned it.

"I don't mind. It was just constant fighting day and night. It was all that ever happened at home."

"I know exactly how that feels, sounds just like my home life," Hayley mentioned while twisting her hair and turning her gaze out the window.

"It will get better. Whatever happens will happen and then the rebuilding starts," Devin appeared to have a good ability to encourage people, "all that matters is how you put the pieces back together. Just promise me you'll never give up."

"Thanks. I'm glad I can open up a little to someone that understands. I promise that I will keep pushing on, only if you promise to try to stop them."

"Absolutely, You deserve better."

Hayley let Devin know the rest of the way to her home. He turned onto Hayley's street and slowly approached the house, turning down the music more as he did.

"Well, here we are, huh?"

"That we are. I had a really good time tonight. Thank you for taking me out, Devin. I'm really happy that I got to see a little into who you really are."

"No problem. I'm always around if you want to talk about it."

"Thanks," Hayley said and sheepishly smiled.

"Have a good night, Hayley."

"I already have," Hayley said with her now familiar shy smile. She leaned over and hugged Devin before getting out of the car.

Hayley walked into the house with a mile wide smile, feeling lighter on her feet than she ever had. Her night went much better than she expected. A night she thought would have no surprises turned out to be the complete opposite. Devin proved to her that he was much more than what he appeared to be. He showed that there was something completely different under his mask. The truth was a much needed and welcome turn of events.

She quietly made her way up to her room to get ready for bed, knowing that she would not be able to sleep for quite a while because of her excitement. She danced through the dark hallway in her socks. As she got to her door, she heard Caroline's door creak and turned to see her sister emerge from the dark room.

"How was your night out with the boy?" Caroline poked.

"It was fine." Hayley mumbled as she attempted to hide her obvious excitement.

"You really expect me to believe that? You're trying so hard not to smile I'm afraid your head might explode." Caroline joked.

"Alright, Alright," Hayley took an excited deep breath, "It was so awesome. He opened up to me so much. He is completely different than I thought and we are much more similar than I would have ever thought."

"That's great, Hayley. It's so nice to see you happy again. It's been way too long since the last time I saw such a big smile on you."

"Thanks, Care. You need to go back to bed now, though, it's late. We can talk more about it later."

"Fine. Goodnight Hayley." Caroline jokingly sulked and slowly turned to make her way back into her room.

"Night, kid."

Hayley changed into her favorite old t-shirt and bright orange running shorts and got into bed. She lay down on her bed and began thinking over the great time she just had. Not being able to sleep, Hayley picked up her journal and began to write. For the first time in months, she finally had something happy to write about. Sitting up in her bed, she penned her newfound happiness down on the page. Her emotions fluttered off her chest, a pleasant change from the anchor that her sadness and frustration had become. She was able to let go of all her negative feelings for a short while and just relax and write. Words began to flow from her heart easier than they had for quite some time. Her ear to ear smile refused to let up as she penned her verse.

How long have the birds been locked
Away in the depths of darkness
Pouring their tears in vain with hopes of being
Pulled free by the eyes of light
Into the sun and warmth of life
Never returning to the hell once known
Eternally shining in the light of
Something strong and golden
Something desired now achieved

Hayley finished her writing and laid down to attempt to get some sort of rest for the night. She slipped one more smile in before drifting off to sleep. A night of dreamless slumber, something Hayley had not had in weeks, finally came. Finally her mind was able to rest for once, if only for a night. Her night was, at last, not filled with the frustrations of the day or nightmares about her family falling apart. Her nightmares had only grown worse as the fighting escalated. The empty slumber was a much needed reprieve for her heart and mind. She awoke in the morning with a cautious optimism that things could actually change in her favor.

The house was a comforting quiet when Hayley woke. Caroline could be heard rustling in the bathroom next door. Hayley wandered out into the hallway and glanced down the stairs. The top of the antique table near the front door sat barren in the morning light. She noticed that her dad's briefcase was not sitting on it like it had nearly every day for as long as she could remember.

Hayley could only hear one person moving around the floor below. The clinking of dishes and the smell of bacon led her to believe that it was her mom. Eli was never much of a cook. He would hardly use anything but the microwave when he was in charge of cooking. Most nights they would just order out. Hayley dragged her feet back into her bedroom and began to slowly get ready.

Caroline came out of the bathroom, bumping into Hayley as she turned toward her room.

"Where's Dad, Care?"

"I don't know," Caroline shrugged, "I haven't seen him since last night. I just assumed he was downstairs somewhere."

"Don't you think it's a little odd that his briefcase is gone?"

"I really don't know. Maybe he left for work already," she turned her body to pass Hayley, "I think you should get ready, though, or we aren't going to have time to eat before we leave."

"Girls, hurry up!" Amy exclaimed.

"See?" Caroline lifted her hand outward, gesturing toward the first floor.

The two girls walked into the kitchen together and took their seats at the table. Amy, with a somber yet frustrated tone, explained that Eli left much earlier than either of the girls thought. While Hayley was out the night before, her parents had had another fight and Eli didn't come home after getting drinks with his friend. Eli spent the night there and told Amy that he did so because he did not want to bother the girls with another night of feuding.

Hayley and Caroline made their way to school. The news of their dad walking out overnight weighed heavily on their minds. Neither could figure out what finally snapped between their parents that would cause that. They had become so accustomed to having both parents at home through the whole split that it was very concerning to each of them that something so drastic happened to cause this fracture. The unorthodox way their parents went about staying in one home through the divorce was done solely to help the girls through it. Eli and Amy were more concerned with keeping as much normalcy as possible for the girls as they could. Only time would tell if it did more harm than good.

When they arrived at school the girls went their separate ways. Her excitement of the previous night out had begun to lighten and be replaced with her usual frustrations and the knowledge that her parents' divorce hearing was drawing ever closer and ever more real. Devin was not around his usual group this day. He kept to himself whenever Hayley caught a glimpse of him in the hallway. *Did he hold up his side of our promise already? Could he actually cause the others to leave me alone?*

The final bell rang throughout the Theroux halls sending the students out into the afternoon sun. Hayley began her walk back to her car, slowly making her way toward Caroline's locker to wait for her. As she turned the last corner she saw Devin across the hall. His glance met her eyes as she smiled at him. He returned with a smile of his own and crossed the hallway to meet her.

"Hey, where have you been all day?" Hayley questioned.

"Getting some extra work done whenever I had some down time. Had to do some catching up for history. Also have, more or less, been avoiding my normal crowd."

"I noticed you weren't around whenever I saw them. I know it's soon but have you had any progress with them yet?"

"No, not really. I haven't had much of a chance to talk to any of them since I've kept to myself all day. I will do what I can, I can't guarantee anything will change for sure though. I don't want them to turn up their intensity on you just cause I told them to leave you alone, ya know?"

"I understand. Thank you for whatever you are able to do, Dev."

"Wait, what are you still doing here anyway?" Devin asked, "You usually leave as soon as the bell rings, don't you?"

"Yeah. Caroline had to stay after a bit today, though." Hayley let little laugh out, "So I get to walk around doing nothing 'til then."

"Oh, I thought maybe you loved school so much you just couldn't bring yourself to leave," Devin chuckled.

"Something like that," Hayley laughed.

"Mind if I hang around with you until she's done?"

"No, not at all," Hayley replied with a blushing smile.

The two of them spent the next half hour talking about their day, joking about school and the upcoming graduation. Hayley found this to be a perfect end to her day. The day felt to be the beginning a new life for her. She was able to coast through the day without any additional stress. Maybe things really were going to change. Caroline worked her way back to her locker and met up with Hayley and Devin. She gave Hayley a quick wry smirk with a raised eyebrow. Hayley's face quickly flushed and knew that it was time to go. She left Devin to return home with a strong, warmhearted smile.

= *5* =

The days began to warm as summer approached. Theroux High School seniors were growing with excitement over the impending graduation. Hayley quickly saw the bittersweet nature of this upcoming change. She would be free from this current prison of fake friends and exile, but would Tulane truly be a new beginning for her? Could it possibly end up just being a continuation of what she had already gone through? Would she have to pretend to be someone else like Devin did? Hayley always feared for the worst about any new situations. Her only real friend and confidant, Caroline, was to be left behind at Theroux. Devin was headed off to Louisiana Tech. Her safety net was going to be pulled further away from her than it had ever been before. She feared that if she fell it would be too far to catch her. Fears of the changes in the coming months consumed Hayley's heart and soul.

Early May arrived in Eden Isle. Every day became warmer than the last. Hayley's emotions grew parallel to the heat of the days. As the temperature rose, her stress and worry also escalated. Her parents' fighting was getting worse every day. The family remained under one roof for the entirety of the collapse of the marriage, apart from a few extra bad days when Eli would stay with friends. Amy refused to move the girls from home and Eli was unable to finalize his new apartment before the court date. The girls both hoped the close proximity would help mend the wounds in the family, but their hopes proved to be for naught.

Hayley continued to escape to her room and books more and more every week. Her desire to escape her current life reached an all-time high. Nothing seemed right to her anymore. Home life had become a living hell. Fighting had become white noise every night. Every day, no matter her overall mood, Hayley always had a hint of anger inside. Most people, especially her family, were never aware of her true emotions. Hayley felt as if she did not know how to be happy anymore.

The day that everyone in the Audige family had dreaded was finally upon them. As the family made their way into the courthouse, Eli from the West end of the parking lot and Amy and the girls from the East, saddened glances were exchanged by all members of the family. Amy and the girls made their way into the courtroom immediately and took their seats. The two girls parked themselves in the front row behind the plaintiff and defendant tables. Eli worked his way in soon after. He slowly and silently took his seat. The time to end the fighting had now arrived.

The proceedings began as the girls quietly observed. Any break in the trial was quickly filled with a deafening silence. A full boring, yet stressful, morning wasted in court resulted in exactly what the girls had expected. Both Hayley and Caroline quietly cried together once the reality finally set in as to what the divorce really meant. The once familiar day trips around town with mom and dad were something of the past and dad would be leaving the only home the family had shared for good. He was off to New Orleans and would be within walking distance from his office. Mom would still be around every day but both girls knew that she would not be the same.

Eli was able to get his apartment the week following the hearing. He was set to leave Eden Isle for New Orleans. A rainy day brought with it the large empty box truck that would soon be filled with all of Eli's things. Hayley and Caroline sat and watched as the house grew increasingly hollow. The movers went in and out of the house for a couple hours like a well-oiled machine, leaving much more empty space than Hayley expected. The sight was very surreal for Hayley. Reality was very difficult for her to comprehend at times. Even watching the truth unfold before her sometimes would not be enough to prove what was really happening. Hayley gave her father one long last tearful hug as he left. She watched until the moving truck drove out of sight, and then made her way back to her room.

Seeing the house look so sparse was very depressing to her as it began to truly show that her dad was leaving. At least he was not too far away, so visiting him would be easy, Hayley thought to herself. Hayley had barely been to New Orleans much despite living so close for so long. Her first visit to Tulane had been the only time she had ever gotten to explore the city. The culture of the city was very enticing to Hayley. She was very excited to be on her own at college and be able to see what New Orleans was really all about.

Her father had only been living there for a week before she was able to visit. He picked her up and they made the short drive to New Orleans together. Caroline was unable to join this time due to a friend's birthday party. Before they went to his apartment he decided to give her the tour of the city. Eli showed her Bourbon Street and the many restaurants and nightlife that it offered. The entire French Quarter was an amazing sight to see. She loved all of the architecture that decorated the city. Her excitement grew more and more with each area they passed. Each street had so much to see and do. The Arts District and many more places and all piqued Hayley's interest and gave her so much to explore more thoroughly once she was there full time. One thing stood out to Hayley as a common theme in some areas of the city, voodoo. These signs and stores were especially intriguing to Hayley. Their strange books, statues, and symbols were so foreign and exciting that she had to know more. Where did it come from? What was it all about?

They continued the tour of the town and made their way past a small group of shops and businesses. A small curio shop, Hallows of Mystery Books and Relics, stood out as the oddity of the group.

Its architecture did not match that of the other buildings around it. It was as if the city was built up around this one shop. Traffic slowed the car to a stop directly in front of the aged building. Hayley was thoroughly inspecting the shop when an old woman slowly made her way out from inside. Her white clothing had been yellowed with age and was visibly tattered. Her dark skin was wrinkled, worn, and sun beaten. Her hair was covered by a cloth head wrap. Hayley stared at this woman as she walked out to the sidewalk in front of the shop. The woman raised her head as if she knew that she was being watched. Hayley quickly shot her gaze away from the woman and looked ahead in the car.

Once she thought that the coast was clear, she turned back only to find the old woman staring right at her. The woman was scowling wide-eyed back at Hayley refusing to break eye contact. She was mumbling something unintelligible as she held her icy watch. Her stare felt like it pierced straight into Hayley's soul. The woman then raised her boney hand and pointed directly at Hayley. She continued her imposing stare as she left her hand hanging in the air, shaking from old age. Hayley only stared back in utter confusion as to why this woman was clearly singling her out amongst the other cars and people on the street. The women's incoherent mumbling continued as Hayley tried to make sense of the entire scenario. *Who is this woman? What does she want?* Hayley could not comprehend what the strange unknown woman could possible want with her.

Finally the traffic picked up and Hayley was able to be torn away from this odd woman and this strange occurrence. Sitting silently, staring at the floor, she was able to make little sense of anything that had happened. Her thoughts raced as she tried to figure out why she was so drawn to this woman and her frightening actions. Try as she might, she was unable to break her own gaze from the woman's darkened eyes. She turned to her dad, who seemed rather oblivious to what had just transpired, and proceeded to ask him what he thought had happened.

"Did you see that old woman outside of the voodoo shop, Dad?"

"I saw her come out of it. Why, what's up?" Eli answered, not breaking his attention from the road.

"She gave me the creepiest stare I have ever seen and pointed at me like I was some freak."

"I'm sure it's nothing, sweetheart. She's probably just trying to drum up curiosity and business for her store. It's a small place so she has to get people in however she can."

"Yeah, I suppose. It's a very creepy way to try to make someone come into your store, though."

"I think you'd be surprised at what some shops will do to get people through the doors," Eli chuckled.

Eli's truck continued down the road as Hayley's mind continued to wander. Nothing seemed to make sense about the little old woman at Hallows. Hayley didn't know her. She had never even seen her. As Hayley and her dad made their way toward his apartment, she couldn't help but continue to think about all of the amazing things she had just seen. Despite the strange occurrence, a new excitement about the upcoming opportunities arose in her heart. She longed to see what each new experience would bring to her.

New places, new knowledge, and most importantly, new people. Her life in Eden Isle was something she wanted to leave behind. Tulane brought so many new chances to start over. She could be anyone she wanted. This thought was incredibly exciting and terrifying at the same time. The image of the strange old woman was burned into Hayley's brain. She was so odd and creepy. She tried blocking the image of the woman's frail, shaking hand out of her mind, but to no avail. It was as if the old woman had some sort of power over Hayley's thoughts.

Eli turned the car around the corner and parked it on the side of the road. Hayley gathered her things and closed the door. She trotted around car and across the street to the large brick apartment building. The neighborhood was basic to say the least. All Hayley could see from the doorstep were small buildings similar to the one her father lived in, a few shops, and a gas station. Eli opened the main door to the building and held it open so that Hayley could pass.

"Thanks, Dad."

Eli hummed a simple acceptance of her thanks and moved himself inside as well. He slowly sauntered over to the elevator, carrying a large box of miscellaneous items he retrieved from the house when he picked up Hayley, and hit the call button with his elbow. The elevator arrived a few short moments later. Its doors opened with a slow smooth motion. Eli stepped inside and motioned with his head for Hayley to come along. As she made her way in to the elevator she began asking questions about the new area in which her dad now lived.

"Dad, what's all of this hoodoo and voodoo stuff about? I saw quite a few things talking about it in the city." Hayley questioned.

"Well, umm I'm not really sure what they're all about, Hay. I pretty much don't know anything about them, short of it was an old religion kind of thing from way back when. I only know what movies have taught me. So I probably know next to nothing about either of them." Eli answered with a concerned yet humorous tone. "I also don't know how much you should get involved with them. They still both sound kind of sketchy to me."

"Oh come on, Dad." Hayley scoffed, "You don't really think that this stuff could actually do anything do you? I mean, how often do you hear about someone being attacked with voodoo. It's not like I'm going to be turned into a frog or something. I'm just curious about it."

"Look, all I'm saying is to be careful. I know you always want to learn about things and that's great, but you still have to be careful. You're my daughter and I don't want anything to happen to you, ya know?" Eli's concern was apparent yet Hayley brushed it off as a father's overprotection.

"I'll keep that in mind," Hayley chuckled. "Thanks, Dad."

Hayley's mind was still racing with thoughts of all of the new places and things she had seen and, for the first time in as long as she could remember, she wasn't afraid of the future. The last time she was this excited was distant memory by now. She pulled a small notebook from her purse and began writing down all the places she wanted to investigate further when she lived in town full time. Audubon Park particularly struck her fancy as a peaceful area to escape the hustle of college and catch her breath for a while. The park held a certain haunting appeal to her - Something so relaxing and so invigorating at the same time. The curio shops in the area caught her eye and drove her imagination wild. She could not decide where to start once she arrived.

The short stop at the apartment before dinner was even shorter than Hayley predicted. Eli took her belongings and tossed them just inside of his apartment door and immediately locked it behind him. The tour Hayley expected was not going to happen now. Eli gestured to Hayley to come along and they made their way back to the car and were back on the road minutes after reaching the apartment. They drove back into the heart of town and stopped off for dinner at a small restaurant.

Bellies full, the two of them headed back to Eli's apartment after dinner and pulled up to the old brick building just as the sun began to descent, darkening the city. They decided to take the stairs this time back up to apartment 3C. Eli's apartment was underwhelming to say the least. It was nothing like their home in Eden Isle. Hayley was very surprised to see how small it was and how cluttered her father had left it. Blank white walls surrounded every room. The carpeting was in less than pristine condition. The one saving grace was that it was a corner unit and received lots of natural light in the evening. This clutter was not the way he had kept his office at home. He had been there a full week and it still looked like he had just brought the boxes in today.

"Dad, no offense, but your place is kind of a mess." Hayley prodded, hoping to get him to take notice and start cleaning up.

"I know, sweetheart, moving in and trying to get work smoothed out again has been a bit rough. I haven't had much of a chance to unpack a lot yet. Anyway, how is school going?"

"Just like it's always been. I can't wait until I'm out here all the time," Hayley stated with clear frustration in her voice. "I want to explore the city a lot more."

"You will love it here. It's a great place." Eli reassured her.

"I think I will, Dad. I feel like I'm supposed to be here, like it's all a part of a bigger, better plan," Hayley muttered, staring with longing out the window at the river in the distance. "Hopefully Tulane will be a lot different than Theroux for me. It's going to be tough being away from Caroline, though. I know she's still close but not having her next door will be tough to get used to."

"Don't worry about it, kid. She's always going to be there anyway."

"I know she will. It's just a comfort thing, ya know?"

"I do. I know exactly what you mean. You and your sister are the ones who are my comfort system now. It's been very hard getting used to not having you right by me anymore. So, are there any boys you're interested in at school?"

"Um..." she turned away from her dad, trying to hide her smile and blushing cheeks, "Well, there is one, his name is Devin.

We went out to eat after my senior show. I've had a crush on him for quite some time now. I don't really have any expectations for anything to start, though. He's going to a different college. We just hung out a little bit."

"Oh come on, Hayley. You've got nothing to lose," Eli bumped Hayley's knee in encouragement, "You're a great girl, you have to let the world see it. I think you should go for it. You never know who sees you the way you see them. Even if it doesn't work, school is almost over anyway so any awkwardness would be short lived. Plus, he may be just as shy about it as you are. His loss."

Hayley chuckled as she shook her head, "Not the greatest motivational speaker are you, Dad?"

"You know what I mean, sweetie. Plus, you look much happier now than I have seen you in a very long time. It's very refreshing to see you smile so much. It will come much easier if you're able to be comfortable with him."

"I know, Dad. I really am happy, first time in a very long time, too. I'm so excited to come live out here. Not just because of Devin. I think it's going to be just what I need. We'll see what happens, though. I don't want to get my hopes up too much."

"You'll definitely like it. I know we didn't come out here much while you were growing up, I wish we had," his voice lowered as he lowered his head, "but with school and your mom and I working all the time, we just didn't get the chance very often. Looking back, we didn't do enough with you girls as a family."

Hayley grabbed her father's shoulder, "Oh, Dad. Don't feel bad about it. We did plenty of stuff together. Caroline and I have still been here a few times with friends, too. Plus, Caroline has a field trip coming up soon to come see a show here. It's kind of a special end of the year kind of thing."

Hayley and Eli stayed by the window to watch the final minutes of the sunset. They talked about the family, school, and the future. Hayley was not used to talking about the family as a broken entity yet. It was a strange thing to her and she could barely bring herself to speak about her mother knowing how it could quickly turn south. Being away from home was an odd experience in itself. Despite her own discomfort of being in a much larger city, she could already feel a connection to the city starting to develop. The allure of New Orleans' culture provided a temptation too strong to resist. Inspiration and curiosity coursed through Hayley's mind with each passing second.

Street lights began to illuminate the ever darkening sidewalks and roadways. Hayley stood up to get a glass of water. As she took her first steps she felt her father's hand grab her arm and heard him clear his throat. "Hayley, listen," his voice was shakier than normal, "I'm really sorry things didn't work out with me and your mom."

"Dad, stop," she continued, fighting through the lump building in her throat, "You don't need to apologize to me about it. Some things just don't work like we think they should. We're all still here and that's what really matters."

"Thanks, kid. I'll always be right here if you need anything. No matter what." He leaned over and gave Hayley a long warm hug before walking away to his room for the night.

The late evening turned to night. Hayley stayed awake thinking about her new home come fall. Though Tulane was not far from Eden Isle, she would still be forced to live as her own person. A new part of her life she badly needed. As she sat on the window sill, she watched the people milling about below the apartment windows. She watched people making their trip home and people just beginning their night. The streets did not empty at night here as they did in Eden Isle. There was so much more life in the big city. Hayley cracked a small smile of excitement as she watched the lights and passing cars of New Orleans. Releasing a heavy yawn, Hayley rose from the window sill and changed into her pajamas. She worked up a makeshift bed on the couch in the living room. Her eyes grew heavier with the fatigue of an exciting, busy day and she drifted off to sleep.

= *6* =

All too quickly the weekend with her father came to a close and Hayley had to go back to Eden Isle and back to reality. Her family, as always, was the lily among the thorns for her. She did not feel any connection to her hometown anymore as she did when she was a young girl. Slowly gathering her things, Hayley got back into Eli's truck. The drive through the humid New Orleans streets tugged on Hayley's mind as she held onto her excitement for the past two days and upcoming year. She had only been in New Orleans for a little over a day yet she was ready to stay there for good. As they drove through the bayous, Hayley felt her phone begin vibrating. She grabbed it from her pocket and saw that it was Caroline calling. Hayley answered, puzzled to hear from her sister whom she would be seeing quite soon.

"Hey Care, what's up?"

"Hi Hayley, do you have a minute?" Caroline's voice had a discernibly sad tone to it.

"Of course. What's wrong? You sound strange." Hayley questioned.

"I'm okay, but I just talked to my friend Sarah. Her grandmother died last week and she's really upset about it," Caroline explained. "She just told me they are planning an estate sale for next week and I offered to help get everything ready for it. Would you be able to help us with it too?"

"Oh that's terrible. Of course I'll help out."

"Thank you. They're trying to get rid of her odds and ends. I think it all happened very suddenly. Sarah never even mentioned anything about her grandmother being sick or anything like that. She did say that her grandma was apparently very interested in some 'dark stuff.' Her parents are convinced that some of her things are somehow tied to her behavior before she died," Caroline continued. "It was all very strange. It didn't really make a lot of sense to me. Anyway, I'll talk to you about it more when you get home. I just wanted to get her an answer quickly. See you soon."

Hayley hung up the phone wondering what Sarah could have meant when she said her grandmother had been interested in "dark stuff." Her mind immediately ventured back to the voodoo shops she had seen with her father and she had a spark of excitement thinking maybe that was it. *How could that cause Sarah's grandma to die?* Hayley's curiosity was once again sparked by the opportunity to learn more about voodoo.

That night Hayley and Caroline went to see Sarah. The girls pulled up to her house and found her outside of her home on the tire swing in the front yard. She sat solemnly on the large rubber tire hanging from the old tree in her front yard, eyes visibly exhausted from tears. The sisters plopped down on the grass with their backs to the tree near the swing and spent the next hour or so talking to her about her grandmother and the events just prior to her passing. Things had been very hard for Sarah and her family due to her grandmother's dwindling health. She had been very close to her ever since her family moved to Eden Isle from Maryland.

Sarah explained to the girls about how strange her grandmother had been acting before she died.

"There were quite a few nights that we could hear her talking to someone in her bedroom. The next morning she never had any recollection of these odd conversations. My parents took her to the doctor to see if there was anything they could figure out about these things going on with her. The only thing the doctor could figure out was that she was beginning to show signs of dementia. He said that it is not uncommon for that sort of thing to happen with elderly people and that we need to keep an eye on her to make sure it didn't worsen or endanger her. I really don't believe that she was just losing her mind. I feel like something was taking her sanity from her. There was never any sign of her mental state getting worse before these last couple weeks."

Sarah's explanation of the incidents surrounding her grandmother stood out as exceptionally odd to Hayley and Caroline. If dementia wasn't causing these things to happen, what was? What did Sarah mean that something was stealing her grandmother's sanity? How could something steal a person's mind? The sisters pleaded with Sarah to keep telling them what was going on just before the death of her grandmother.

"Strange things started happening at her home. The smoke detector in her room had been set off multiple times in the last couple weeks. Although any time I would rush in there to check on her, no smoke at all was in the air. You could smell that something had been burned but there were no signs of any burns anywhere," Sarah continued. "The night before my grandmother died; there was a huge boom that shook the entire house. It was like a cannon went off inside the house. The whole family ran to her room and we found that the window had been shattered and that everything had been blown outward from the center of the room. We found grandma knocked out in the corner. She had a lighter in her hand when we found her. She had no use for one either, she wasn't a smoker. The only thing we really found was a big dust pile in the middle of the room that looked like a piece of chalk exploded."

"That is really strange, Sarah. Have you looked into what could have happened?" Hayley questioned.

"We asked around and no one had ever heard of those kind of things happening."

"I can imagine it would be difficult to find information about something like that," Caroline added. "You may want to check some old books at the library or look online. It might help make sense of this."

"Yeah, I've thought about doing that. I just don't even know where to begin," Sarah went on to explain the things they had found after the incident. "The way the window broke was very weird. Only the glass broke out, no pieces landed inside. The wood and wall around it weren't even touched. After we got grandma out, I started searching around her room trying to figure things out. I found some old voodoo dolls she had had for quite some time. I remember seeing them a few times in the last few years. There was an old notebook on the floor in front of her night stand. I flipped through it and the whole thing was empty. It was a little weird to me considering how old it looked. It had strange symbols all over the front with a big stone on the cover. I have no idea what the symbols mean."

"I see what you mean about not knowing where to start," Hayley intently listened while trying to make sense of what she was being told.

"We've started putting her things together for the sale. Mostly things that aren't sentimental to us. Some of the weirder things she had are already packed up for the sale. We just want to get that stuff out of here as soon as possible. It gives us all the creeps."

"I don't blame you for wanting it out. It is a bit unnerving even thinking about it. We will be here to help with the sale Saturday. If you need anything at all, don't hesitate to call me or Caroline."

"Thank you so much, girls. I really appreciate it. I should get inside, though, it's getting late. I'll talk to you soon," Sarah got up from her swing and headed into her house.

The girls went home that night with minds full of wonder about this mysterious woman they never got the chance to meet. Hayley felt as though she needed to find out more about this woman. It seemed like there was more about her that was not being told. She lay awake staring at her ceiling trying to figure out the best way to get information about Sarah's grandmother. Working out how to be Sherlock Holmes without seeming too nosey was proving to be extremely difficult. She finally decided that digging and snooping was not the way to go. Hayley decided she would just ask Sarah what she thought had happened the next time she ran into her.

The following days after school, Sarah was nowhere to be found. Hayley stayed longer than normal trying to find her and attempt to get to the bottom of the occurrences surrounding her grandmother. Attempting to keep her search secret, Hayley was unable to ask Caroline for Sarah's phone number. The school week passed without a single chance to dig deeper into her quest of information.

= 7 =

The day of the estate sale arrived and Hayley was at last able to speak to Sarah again. The short driveway was lined with boxes of clothes and knick-knacks. Amongst the boxes and piles of junk, there were also some curious items. Strange books, dolls, and beads all caught Hayley's attention. One item in particular stuck out amongst the clutter. A strange notebook buried and hidden under novels and an old bible in a small box. This particular notebook appeared to be extremely old. The dark brown leather cover was dry and cracked. Its binding was beginning to split but was still very strong. *This had to be the book Sarah was talking about.* The pages inside were yellowed and very dusty. Just as Sarah said, the book was completely empty, every page was barren. The cover of this notebook was covered in strange symbols that Hayley had never seen before. In the center of the cover, surrounded by symbols and stitching was a large stone. The oval stone was a beautiful deep ebony color. The stone appeared to be in pristine condition despite the very rugged appearance of the rest of the notebook. Its deep color gave hints of deep reds and blues in the bright sun. The colors glowed through the darkness of the stone. This strange book was clearly much older than Hayley had imagined.

The estate sale lasted into the late afternoon. People came and went, picking through the piles with minimal interest. A few household items were purchased while most of the odd and ends remained untouched. The taboo nature of the things being sold must have scared off some people as most wouldn't even go near the table to look at them. Sarah and her mom decided to donate all of the unsold items to whatever charity would be willing to take them the following week.

The girls began sorting and boxing the items again, one by one, and moving them back into the garage. Messily stuck in a pile of vintage voodoo books was the strange notebook. Hayley plucked it out with a bit of relief seeing that it had not been sold. She picked it up and began examining its features again.

"Hey Sarah, is this the book you were talking about the other night?" Hayley asked. She knew the answer already but needed a way to get Sarah talking about her mysterious grandmother.

"Yeah that's the one. It's really weird isn't it?"

"Definitely. Have you found out what it is yet?"

"No, but my parents said that Grandma had it as long as they could remember. I remember them saying she got it from some old book store when she was traveling the Caribbean a long time ago."

"I see," Hayley wasn't satisfied with that as the whole answer. She continued to prod Sarah for more information. "What was she doing in the Caribbean?"

"Umm, just traveling, I think. She used to go all over the place while she was still healthy. Mom and Dad told me that she was always interested in voodoo and whatnot and would look for new and bizarre information about it. I think a lot of her things here are from her trips... Now that I think about it, that's probably why Mom wants all of this stuff out. She never believed in what Grandma did. I remember them getting into some arguments about the things she brought back. Mom always said that she didn't want

Grandma getting those ideas in my head. She didn't think that my grandma was a good influence on me."

"What ideas did she not want to put in your head?" Hayley questioned. "Voodoo stuff?"

"Yeah. She thought that it wouldn't be a healthy thing for me to get interested in," Sarah laughed. "Sometimes I think she would prefer that I wear a suit of bubble wrap so I couldn't get hurt."

Hayley giggled and continued looking over the book. She began to feel a connection to it as she felt the warm leather in her hands. The more she held and inspected the book, the more she felt she needed to have it, "So would you mind if I bought it from you?"

"Are you serious? You really want that thing?"

"Yeah, I think it's really interesting."

"Well in that case, just take it. I don't really see anyone else coming around and wanting that, we were just going to donate it anyway."

"Really? That's awesome, thanks, Sarah!" Hayley was ecstatic. She would now be able to take the book and hopefully find out where it came from, or at the very least find out some sort of information about it. The book's warm leather seemed to meld with Hayley's hands. Something about holding it just felt right, like she was meant to have it. She had only known of the book for a very short time, yet she felt as if she had had it for years and knew every detail of it by heart. The book felt as if it was giving off an energy that Hayley could sense flowing through her body. Knowing that Caroline would not believe what she was feeling, she put the book into her bag and hid it away in her desk as soon as she got home.

After preparing for bed, Hayley took the book out of its hiding place and again flipped through its empty yellowed pages. With each turn of the page she could smell the remnants of old dust and smoke. Hayley rifled through the last few pages and turned back to the first page. Every page was completely unmarked with the exception of the very first page. She found that it had worn imprints of old writing on it. *Where was the page the writing was on?* The book showed no signs of any pages being torn out. Despite her confusion and wonder, Hayley grew too tired to stay awake. She placed the book on her nightstand and slipped off to sleep.

= *8* =

Hayley awoke covered in a boiling sweat, her room glowing a bright orange. She shook the sleep from her eyes to find her desk and TV engulfed in flames. Jumping from her bed she landed upon a charred, ash covered floor. Hayley collapsed to her knees and lifted her head again to see deep black smoke emanating from her walls and window. As she kneeled, horrified, she saw the walls begin to tear open. Flames poured into the room as two unknown beings come through the walls. The creatures looked to be gnarled versions of humans in appearance. Their gaunt human features had been twisted and exaggerated into something awful. Each had skin of tainted gray, elongated legs with knees that bent backwards, and rawboned hands. They crawled through the holes with slow, haunting motions. She dropped her head into her hands to hide the terrible sight ahead of her.

Hayley, still shaking, forced herself to lift her head only to find that she was face to face with the horrifying creature. She jolted back against the wall. Its grotesque face was only exacerbated by twisted, broken horns growing from its head. Its eyes were opaque pools of black. The creature's stunted nose fluttered as it smelled its surroundings. As it leaned ever closer to Hayley it began twisting and turning its head as it appeared to examine her, although its gaze appeared to look straight through her. Hayley felt the creature slowly run its cold, seemingly lifeless hand down her cheek. She felt its broken nails scrape her skin as she tried with all of her power to remain still. Sensing her fear, it reared back and released a blood curdling, otherworldly, scream. Black smoke poured from its mouth as it let out the horrible cry. Dropping its head back down, the beast looked to the wall to the side of Hayley, appearing to lose sight of her.

Hayley felt a small flash of clarity as she realized that the creatures must be blind. Hayley crumpled back to the floor silently and lied motionless. A few short moments seemed like an eternity. Hayley attempted to gather her emotions and slowly slid to her night stand. Hearing the two creatures' feet and nails scraping along the floor, she lifted her gaze to see them exiting her room through the torn walls. Her eyes peeked along the opposite wall to find a singular flame working its way across the wall. It appeared to be spelling out words as it moved. Hayley followed the burning trail and watched as the words *ASH BURNS WITHIN* were scorched into the wall. As soon as she read the words quietly to herself the entire room exploded in flames.

In a flash, Hayley jolted awake from her nightmare. The morning sun gave her room a peaceful warmth. She broke down in tears again. This time her tears were a mix of remaining fear and happiness in the recognition that her ordeal was not a terrifying reality. Before she could gain her composure, she heard the sound of footsteps coming across the hall. Hayley sharply jumped, nearly falling out of her bed, when Caroline knocked on her door. She peeked around the door with a concerned glance.

"You okay, Hayley? I could hear you crying."

"No." Hayley sighed, sitting with her hands on her head and fighting back more tears, "I had the worst nightmare I've ever had. It was so scary and felt so real."

"Aww, it's okay, Hay, everything is fine. What happened?"

Hayley began to describe her nightmare to Caroline, giving every detail that she could remember. Even knowing it was over, she still became frightened thinking about it again. She described the horrible creatures that she encountered. "I have no idea what any of it could mean. I hope I never have something like that again."

"That's definitely freaky. I'm sure it's nothing, though. It's probably just your mind being too active while you sleep. Don't let it get to you."

"Yeah, you're probably right," Hayley admitted, beginning to get off of her bed. She began her morning routine as she did every day, however, today was different. Her emotions ran wild. She became very nervous and jumpy after her awful night. Each creak of the house and closing door sent shockwaves through her entire body. This day was bound to be a very long one.

Hayley arrived at school still trying to shake off the after effects of her night. She trekked through the halls to her first class. Nothing could separate her mind from the thoughts trapped inside her nightmare and the mysterious book she left behind. Something in the back of her mind remained with that book, like a voice calling out to her. Her thoughts stayed hooked on the barren yet cryptic pages. Classes quickly failed to gain any of Hayley's attention on this day. Lectures and lesson plans played out as background noise to the ongoing mystery of her nightmares.

The only respite of Hayley's mental runaround came as soon as she walked into chemistry. The experiments required her full attention and participation. She sparked her Bunsen burner and began filling her beakers. The necessary concentration was a welcome change for her today. She noted her findings and continued her work. As soon as she got into her work groove, Hayley soon found her mind drifting to the book again. She could not wait to get home and inspect it some more. Excitement soon gave way to fear as Hayley saw motion out of the corner of her eye. She looked toward the flame of the burner and within its flickering saw something. Leaning closer she saw that the blurry image was something she recognized. Alex, Hayley's partner, looked over to see Hayley leaning closer and closer to the flame.

"What are you doing, Hayley?" Alex questioned as she nudged her.

"Huh? Oh, um, nothing. Just spaced out a bit, I guess."

"Well wake up, brainiac. You just about set your hair on fire," Alex snickered.

Hayley quietly smiled and shook off her distraction. When Alex looked away again, she started studying the flame once more. The figure inside the flame had become much clearer than it looked seconds before. Slowly Hayley realized that it was one of the creatures from her nightmare. The creature twisted around to stare into Hayley's eyes, contorting its neck to do so. The beast then reared back and leapt straight out of the flame at Hayley. Letting out a frightened yelp she quickly jumped out of her chair and away from the table.

"Hayley! What's the problem?" Mrs. Florence barked out, causing Hayley to snap back to reality.

"Sorry, I just, um, burned myself," Hayley falsely confessed, not wanting to draw more attention to herself with the truth.

"Well get it together and keep it down. It's not safe to startle everyone with the burners on."

"Sorry, Mrs. Florence," Hayley sulked back into her seat, shaking her head from embarrassment. Her heart was still racing when she returned to her work. *What in the world is going on?*

Why am I still seeing these creatures even though I am awake?
Keeping her incident a secret from everyone became increasingly difficult as the day wore on. The other students' confused and judging stares thickened the air of the classroom. The bell rang to Hayley's relief and the class filed out of the room. Hayley sluggishly packed her things into her bag, still embarrassed from her in-class episode. After the final bell sounded, Hayley silently and deliberately made her way to the car to meet Caroline. She found her sitting on the hood of the car reading her book.

"Let's go," Hayley commanded without even a simple greeting.

"What's wrong with you?" Caroline shot back, not lifting her head from her book.

"Just get in the car. I don't want to talk about it."

Caroline shrugged it off and the girls began the drive home without saying another word to one another. The silence inside the car became deafening. Hayley's embarrassment from school spiraled into frustration and anger. With every passing second, she gripped the steering wheel tighter, turning her knuckles bone white. The light ahead changed to red and Hayley pulled the car to a stop. She closed her eyes and took a deep breath.

"I'm sorry about earlier. I was just ticked off from school today."

"That's okay, Hay. Do you want to talk about it?"

"There isn't really a lot to talk about. I just made myself look like an idiot in front of the whole class today. I lost focus on what I was doing and scared myself, but yelled in the middle of class in the process. "

"Oh," Caroline jawed, trying to hold off a grin, "so what scared you?"

"I don't really know how to explain it. I saw the thing from my dream again. That weird person thing with horns, you know? I don't get why I'm still seeing it now that I'm awake."

"Ah, I wouldn't look too much into it," Caroline shook her head, "I'm sure you're just thinking about it still because it scared you so much last night. I've seen pieces of my own dreams while I'm awake too."

"Yeah, you're probably right. Oh well." Hayley pulled the car into the driveway at home as they wrapped up their conversation. Both girls exited the car and made their way inside. Caroline went straight to her homework in the living room. Hayley set her backpack on the floor near the end table in the front hallway. She headed right up to her room and over to her desk to grab the notebook. The book's hiding place was empty. Digging around the other drawers she found that the notebook was nowhere to be found in the desk. At this point she began to worry that her mom had possibly thrown the book away. Its appearance was not that of a cherished item. Amy would absolutely and without question dispose of a tattered old blank notebook.

Hayley turned toward her bed and saw that the notebook was sitting the end table to the left of her bed. With a sigh of relief she picked up the book. The cover was warm and inviting. The pages felt frail yet strong at the same time. Opening the worn cover, she saw that the missing text from the second page was now visible. The sight of the once invisible words shocked her. Once she was able to regain her focus, she tried to understand the sloppy writing and make sense of its words. Squinting and turning the book was not helping to clarify the blurred and slightly smudged letters on its pages. Finally Hayley was able to work out what she believed was scribbled on the paper.

From courage to shame;

All are changed within the flame

Two lines. She read two simple lines, however, they might as well have been written in a foreign language. *What a puzzling statement. What did it mean? How could a flame change someone?* Nothing about the two lines stood out as a clue to its meaning. Hayley took out a separate notebook and wrote the passage down. She thoroughly examined the lines and separated each word. There were no hidden terms in the first letters, no apparent wordplay involved, and secret order to the words or letters. Every covert technique, no matter how obscure, seemed to come up empty for a possible answer to the verse.

Hayley thought that Caroline could possibly have some insight as to what these words could mean. She walked down to the living room where she found her sister working on her paper. She pulled up a chair and placed the paper on top of her sister's hands on the keyboard. Caroline raised an eyebrow and glanced at Hayley out of the corner of her eye.

"Can I help you?" She said with a smirk.

"I need some help. What do you think this means?" Hayley pointed to the paper she placed by her sister.

Caroline read the passage out loud, then again in her head. She stared at the passage and wrinkled her brow in confusion.

"Is this all that there is to it? I feel like something is missing from this. You know, like, context," Caroline giggled. Hayley was not amused and shook her head.

"The notebook I got from Sarah was empty when I got it. It was empty when looked through it last night. It was empty when I went to school. When I got home this was written in it. Did you sneak in and write in it?"

"I haven't even seen the book since you got it. So, no. I have never touched it."

"That's so creepy. Where do you think it came from, Care?"

"Is it possible that you just missed it when you flipped though it before?"

"There's no way. I've looked through that thing like twelve times already. Every page has been empty every time."

Caroline sat back in her chair away from her computer. She picked up the paper again to look at the passage. "Can you show me the real one?"

Hayley nodded and proceeded to go up to her room and grab the notebook. She came back down to the living room, notebook in hand, opening it to the passage. Handing the book to Caroline, Hayley could see the growing confusion on her sister's face. Caroline set the book on the table and leaned very close to it. She examined the writing on the page, looking for any sign of oddities.

"Are you sure that's what this thing says? It's very hard to read. Whoever did it needs to practice writing or has a very shaky hand."

"I really can't be totally sure, but I studied that book for so long last night and now this," Hayley said, shrugging her shoulders, "I can't think of anything else that it could say. You can easily make out some of the words. Flame is definitely there."

"Absolutely. I don't really see anything else that could be either. So what are you going to do about it?"

"What else can I do?" Hayley began to laugh, "It's not like I can call in the CSI team to look it over."

Caroline smiled and gave the notebook back to Hayley. Hayley went back to her room to try and find some morsel of information about the text. Scouring and digging on the internet yielded no results, not even a simple hint. Growing increasingly frustrated with the lack of new knowledge on the mysterious verse, Hayley took the book and forcefully threw it into her desk drawer. With a deep huff she slammed the drawer closed. The loud slam was audible through the entire house. Caroline got up from her chair to see what the ruckus was all about.

"You okay up there, Hay?"

"Yeah," Hayley replied with a discernible frustration in her voice, "I just want to figure out this stupid page!"

"Just let it go for a while. It will probably come to you later."

"Fine." Hayley dropped the subject for the time being. Her irritation had finally boiled over. She left her room mumbling her frustrations, leaving the book behind in the desk. Once Hayley had calmed down, she sat down to finish her homework. Her work helped distract her mind from the book for a couple hours.

"Girls, dinner time!" Amy bellowed throughout the house. Hayley and Caroline came into the dining room together to eat.

The three ladies sat quietly around the table. Conversation came at a premium this night. Caroline and Amy chatted briefly about school and Amy's work. Hayley ate in silence, wanting nothing to do with any conversation. Most questions asked of her went answered only by a sentence or two. Growing more and more frustrated with the dragging silence and slow moving meal, Hayley quickly finished her food and excused herself from the table.

With a deep thump, Hayley flopped down on her bed. Her tawny hair bounced off the pillow as she dropped her head. She closed her eyes and dozed off for a few moments. When she awoke she had turned onto her side and was staring at her cluttered desk. Knowing what was inside of that desk threw her mind into a whirlwind of curiosity and frustration. Her gaze did not waver from the drawer containing the book. One question ran around Hayley's mind. *Do I dare try and figure out the passage again?*

= *9* =

Curiosity again had won out over logic. With a heavy sigh, Hayley drug herself to the desk and plucked the book from the drawer. The scent of the fire pit rolled through Hayley's window. A small grin peeked out from her pursed lips. The crackling wood and soft smoky aroma were comforting to her. Looking out of her window, she found that Caroline had already made her way out to the pit.

Hayley took her seat near the edge of the pit and pulled the book from her bag. She blocked the book from Caroline's sight, not wanting to hear any criticism about her stubbornness. She closed her eyes and breathed in the warm air emanating from the fire. A small bit of tranquility washed over her mind as she sat back in her chair.

Caroline awkwardly rustled through her papers on the opposite side of the fire pit. She glanced up at Hayley every couple minutes, hoping to spark up a conversation.

"So, have you figured out that page yet?"

"Not even close," Hayley chuffed, "I'm no closer now than I was when I found it. It's driving me crazy."

"Oh well, I would have to think it doesn't mean anything. Apart from it probably being a metaphor, I've got nothing."

"Yeah, must be," Hayley shook her head and peered down at the book in her lap.

Amy poked her head out of the back door and looked to the girls, she had Caroline's cell phone in her hand, "Caroline, your phone keeps ringing, please come answer it."

"Sure, Mom," Caroline jumped up from her seat and trotted into the house.

Hayley waited until Caroline was out of sight to open the book again. She went back to her familiar glazed over stare at the page, falling back into pure confusion. Shifting her seat closer to the fire she lifted the page to the golden fire's light. A strange thing happened when the fire light hit the page. The edges of the page appeared to gain a rich smoky hue, providing a blackened frame for the passage. The letters grew clearer once backlit with the fire. Hayley's decoding of the scribbled message was entirely correct. Not a single letter on the page was clouded anymore. Unfortunately, an answer to the verse was not revealed by the new spotlight. Hayley, completely fed up with her stagnant search, ripped the page out of the book. The brittle paper tore with minimal resistance. Dust fell from the book as the page was pulled from the spine.

Hayley brushed the dust off of her lap and gave the page one last inspection before giving up. Nothing became evident even with the changes the light brought. Taking the page in her left hand, Hayley crushed it into her right hand and shaped it into a brittle crinkled ball. She cursed the page as she tossed it into the fire and watched it drop into the flames. A light sense of relief and satisfaction came from destroying the page. Hayley tucked the book back into her bag and moved on to reading. She skimmed through a few sentences and glanced back to the fire pit. To her surprise, the page had not yet ignited. Moving the ball deeper into the embers of the pit also failed to bring the page to combustion.

The page sat still inside the fire, the thin edges not even being burned by the very high temperature inside the pit. Hayley shrugged her shoulders and looked back to her book.

A loud spark pop came from the flames and perked Hayley's ears. She looked at the flames and saw the page starting to shift. The outer edge of the paper ball began expanding outward and getting singed. Edges began to glow bright orange and the page began getting consumed by the flames. As the page grew hotter and hotter, the flames surrounding it began changing color. The bright oranges and reds shifted to bright green, the kind of green that appears when copper is burned. The green flames burned in the center of the pit like the iris of an eye. The page twisted as it burned in its emerald oven. Hayley watched the beautiful colors and saw that the flames began to twist and swirl around the page. The flaming funnel rose out of the fire pit higher than Hayley's head. More and more sparks began coming from the page and its embers. As the page burned the smoke coming from it increased. The tower of fire spun faster and began expanding. Suddenly the green flames rapidly grew outward and came crashing down into themselves giving off a resounding boom that shook Hayley to her core and knocked her out of her chair.

Everything went black. The fire, gone. The pit, gone. The house, trees, Caroline, Mom, all gone. A dim light began to glow in a distant fog. The light revealed the silhouette of a street light. A small object sat on the ground under the lamp. The warm glow drew Hayley to her feet. She clumsily stumbled forward a few steps, looking for something to brace against. After a few unsure steps she was able to muster enough balance to continue toward the distant light. With each rough step the street light appeared to move farther away. The faint light flickered in the distance. Hayley's uneasy walk grew to a cautious jog. Sounds of footsteps and breathing began coming from unseen bodies in the blackness. A desperate sweat rushed over Hayley's face. Her run, now broken from fear, came to a complete stop. She dropped to her knees and peered toward the light in dejection and terror.

"Give in," a haunting whisper broke out from the darkness, "and burn where you lie."

"No," Hayley muttered defiantly. Her voice no longer sounded light like that of a young lady, but deep and coarse and not human. Pain and anger flowed from her breath like the fire of a dragon, "I'm done hiding. It's time to fight back." Dust flew off the ground as she slammed her fist onto the ground. Hayley began to pull herself back to her feet. Her eyes no longer burned from tears, but burned from the rage in her heart. She propped herself up on one knee, letting out a powerful breath.

A crackling noise rumbled under the earth. The dirt shifted and cracked under her knee. With simultaneous forceful thrusts, two hands burst from the ground and grabbed Hayley's ankles. Flames erupted from the ground surrounding the hands. The pale dry skin of the hands was cracked and bleeding, nails broken and yellowed, pulling at her skin, ripping her tender flesh. The pain quickly dropped Hayley back to two knees on the ground. Cries of pain stifled only by the anger growing inside of her. Hayley repeatedly slammed her fist into the hand holding her left ankle to the ground. The bloodied hand retreated back into the ground followed by an otherworldly screech. The second hand dragged her foot along the ground, turning and scraping the ankle against the rough earth. Hayley attempted to climb to her feet but was pulled back down on her rear end by a harsh forward wrench by the blood-spattered hand. Mustering a little more strength, Hayley was able to prop herself up on her hands and stomp on the hand with enough force to break free of its grasp.

With the demon hands now gone, Hayley slowly stood up. Sweating and breathing heavily, she ignored the immense pain from her bleeding ankle. She turned to the lonely light post. The once distant lamp now stood no more than fifty feet from her. The small object beneath the lamp revealed itself as the old notebook. The pain in her wounded ankle would not deter her from reaching the light, nothing would. Smoke rose from under the notebook, completely hiding it from sight. Hayley stared as the smoke rose higher and blocked out the light. Her stare was then disrupted by the deep rumbling growl of an unseen creature. Fear exploded in Hayley's heart.

After the smoke dissipated the golden light remained broken by a dark figure standing in the glow. The book had disappeared. It was a massive creature, easily eight feet tall. The figure's arms were long and lanky. Its legs bent backward at the knee. Details of its face were hidden in shadow. Its raspy breathing sounded like that of a heavy smoker, scratchy and trying. The beast then turned toward Hayley, revealing a second head previously hidden by the first. The growl of the creature was deeper than any animal Hayley knew. Still on her knees, Hayley shook with fear. The monster grabbed the lamp post, instantly blowing out the bulb at the top with only its touch. The only thing keeping the creature visible was now gone. All light had vanished. As Hayley stared into the void, four piercing orange glowing eyes appeared near where the lamp once was. With each movement, the eyes left dimly glowing trails in the darkness. The creature was still looking right at her. The eyes soon began to shake and, just as fast as they appeared, vanished.

In a daze, Hayley woke up on the ground next to the fire pit. She rose from the ground with a terrible headache. *What in the world just happened? How long was I out?* Slowly she worked back into her chair and tried to wrap her head around the event. She looked into the fire and saw that the page was now completely gone. The glaring light of the fire hurt Hayley's eyes. Leaning back in her chair, she strongly closed her eyes and rubbed her temples as her headache grew worse. She looked to her feet and saw that both ankles were completely fine. Not a single scratch on either. Dropping her head into her palms, she tried to hide the sound of her sobs.

The sound of the back door opening brought her back to reality. Caroline closed the door behind her and walked back to the fire. She returned to the fire pit and found her sister looking very distraught. Hayley heard Caroline coming back outside and attempted to hide any signs of her emotions.

"Hayley are you okay?" Caroline asked while increasing the pace of her steps.

"Care, where have you been for so long?"

"What are you talking about? I was in the house for no more than five minutes," Caroline confusedly replied.

"That's impossible. Did you not just hear a huge boom?"

"What? No, definitely not. I was right inside the door the whole time. All I saw was you tip over in your chair. That was right before I came back outside."

"It doesn't make sense. I just threw that page into the fire and it just like exploded. It was crazy, like a tornado of smoke and then BOOM. It knocked me completely out of my chair and I just woke up from it. I had to be out for at least twenty minutes."

"Seriously, Hayley. I was inside for no more than five minutes at the most," Caroline explained, "nothing even looks different at all out here. You sure you're feeling okay? I was standing just inside and didn't hear or see anything going on out here."

Hayley shook her head. She could not believe that Caroline didn't notice anything. The blast could not have gone unnoticed, it was far too big and far too loud. The pounding in her head was just as loud as the blast. *How did Caroline not hear the explosion? Did it actually happen? How did I get a headache if it didn't happen? What was that thing under the street light?*

What is wrong with me?

The gold hands of Hayley's watch glimmered in the fire's warm glow. 9:17. *Caroline was right. There's no way that this vision lasted more than a few minutes. It felt like an eternity.* Caroline continued to plug away at her homework across the fire pit. A tepid breeze rolled through the backyard as Hayley climbed from her seat. She rubbed her eyes and tried to shake some of the confusion from her head.

"I'm going to go lie down," Hayley quietly said as she began walking away from the fire pit.

"Are you okay, Hay?"

Hayley didn't answer, only gave a vague hand wave as she left. She walked into the house holding and shaking her head. Caroline sat back in her chair, beginning to genuinely worry about her sister's well being. The door slowly swung behind Hayley as she entered the house, remaining ajar from her weak push. Amy turned and watched as Hayley shuffled in behind her.

"Are you alright, sweetie?" Amy questioned, "You seem pretty frazzled."

Hayley managed only a mumbled answer and nodded her head. She braced herself on the railing as she turned to face the staircase. The stairs to her room never seemed so insurmountable as they did at this time. The simple fourteen stairs might as well have been well over a hundred. Staggering and stumbling clumsily up the stairs, Hayley began to sweat and breathe heavily. Her vision began to blur and turn. She stretched for her door, missing her first two attempts. Hayley dragged her bag across the floor, leaving it near her desk, shuffled over to her bed, and dropped herself onto it staring at the ceiling.

A strange dark motion appeared in Hayley's peripheral. She looked over toward her door, squinting through the dimly lit room to see deep black smoke seeping through her door frame. Smoke spilled into the room, rising to the ceiling and sinking to the floor. Wide-eyed, Hayley's breathing began to quicken and her nerves quivered. Franticly she felt and fumbled for the light switch of her table lamp. The white light flooded the room, expelling the darkness from every corner. Hayley looked back to the door only to find that the smoke was completely gone. In one instant it had vanished. She let out a large sigh of relief. Her headache flared as she shook the hallucination from her mind. Hayley winced as she lay herself back down on her pillow.

I'm okay. It was nothing. It was just shadows, there's nothing there. Only my mind fooling with me.

It became obvious that sleep would not come easy on this night. Finding a diamond on a beach of rhinestones would have been easier for Hayley at this point. Frustration boiled under her skin as she tossed and turned. She picked up a book from her nightstand and began reading, hoping it would calm her mind and nerves. Her focus on the book was disrupted by a small flicker of motion off to her side. Glancing over her left shoulder she could find nothing even slightly moving. Shrugging off the event, Hayley went back to reading. Her reading was once again interrupted by another peek of movement to the same side. Hayley ignored it. The movement happened again and was accompanied by a small rustling noise. She could not ignore it now.

With a strong thud she slammed her book closed, tossed it aside, and looked toward the wall once more. Again she saw nothing moving. The rustling noise sounded again, but behind her this time. She quickly spun around and to her horrified surprise saw the painted phoenix on her wall turning its head around the room. Its black painted figure turned to ebony feathers as it pulled away from the wall. The phoenix turned its head to face Hayley. Upon the sight of her its eyes burst into flames and the dark bird let out an ear splitting shriek. As the phoenix began to pull itself out of the wall, it dug its talons into the wall and pushed off, leaving large gashes in the drywall. The midnight bird tore itself from the wall and began to soar around the room, leaving a trail of fire burning in its wake. The wind off the phoenix's wings blew Hayley's hair over her shoulders.

Again the bird turned to face Hayley, letting out another piercing shriek. The fire in its eyes intensified as it tilted its head toward her. The ebony beast gave a powerful thrust of its wings pushing itself backward in the air. It flew upward and shot forward toward Hayley. As it dove, the phoenix pushed its talons in front of its body. Hayley dropped back on her bed to avoid the phoenix's attack, but the creature shifted its path to ensure a clean strike. Hayley's heart raced as the phoenix grew closer. The razor sharp claws growing nearer by the second. A silent scream escaped her lungs. Her breath shook as she quivered with fear. Nightmarish thoughts of her flesh being torn from her face by the evil bird raced through her mind. The moment before the claws pierced Hayley's face, a large cloud of smoke rushed over her body. She opened her eyes and the phoenix was gone.

The smell of smoke lingered over Hayley's bed. The black fog from the bird had dispersed and completely faded away. Hayley's sweat from the heat of the flames vanished. The painted phoenix on the wall appeared once again in its original position.

No evidence of anything that had just happened was left in the room. The claw marks left when the phoenix dug in to push of the wall were nowhere to be found. She lay on her bed facing the ceiling trying in vain to catch her breath and regain her composure. Her eyes began to burn as she held back her tears. The tears did not escape on this night.

Hayley lay with her insomnia holding her prisoner. Nothing she did could bring her the slumber she so desired. Reading did nothing to calm her mind. She saw the words on the page but nothing set in. Eyes glazed over, she turned to her side and looked out the nearby window. A lone street light glowed in the distance. Her eyes widened as she connected that it was the lamp from her vision at the fire pit. Hayley's breathing hastened as she peered at the light on the corner. Unable to slow her heart rate, she flipped over to her other side and gazed at her desk. The sight of the empty chair gave Hayley a small piece of relaxation amongst the current chaos. The chair reminded her of comfort and home and began to slow her heart rate back to its normal pace. She let out a long drawn breath and grabbed her book once more, maybe she could focus this time.

One chapter. Two chapters. Three chapters became six chapters. Her heart was calmed yet she could not sleep. The hours passed and Hayley remained awake on her bed. Frustration brewed in the back of her mind. She grabbed the remote control on her nightstand and turned on her T.V. The glow of the screen gave a cool azure hue to the room. Infomercials selling pots and pans, weight loss, and cosmetics bombarded her. *What time is it?* Hayley's mouth fell agape when she saw the time on her clock. 5:38 A.M. The whole night was gone. Not one minute of sleep the entire night. Her alarm would be going off in less than two hours. Hayley groaned as she rolled over onto her back and placed her hands on her forehead. Her mind grinding, she closed her eyes and breathed deeply. The dim bloom of the rising sun gave birth to a new day as Hayley finally faded into a shallow sleep.

= 10 =

The irritating buzzing of Hayley's alarm clock shook her back to consciousness. Her rude awakening was exacerbated by the bright morning sun shining in her face. She squinted and held her hand over her eyes as she fumbled for the off button on the alarm clock. Her face cooled in the shadow of her hand and she was able to open her eyes wider. Birds could be heard chirping outside of her window. The house was silent this morning. Not even the quiet clinking of dishes could be heard. *Caroline must still be asleep. I should see if she noticed anything odd last night.* Breaking her deliriousness proved to be more difficult than most days. Her feet landed on the floor next to her bed like large stones. She rubbed her eyes and lazily rose to her feet. The soft carpet caressed her bare toes, comforting her mind. She dragged her feet all the way to the bathroom to prepare for what would surely be a very long day.

She grabbed her toothbrush and turned on the faucet. Sounds of motion could be heard coming from Caroline's room, feet creaking on the floor. Hayley turned off the water and set her toothbrush down to wait for Caroline to come in. A moment later Caroline entered the bathroom. "Good morning, Hay – Whoa," she cut herself off, "you look like you got hit by a bus," Caroline blurted out.

Hayley kept quiet for a moment before responding. Her disheveled hair and exhausted eyes were the polar opposite of Caroline's bright and cheery appearance this morning. "I'm sure I do look like that, I feel like it too," she lowered her eyes to the sink, "I barely slept at all last night. I just couldn't relax after leaving the fire. Did you notice anything out of the ordinary with me or anything outside?"

"Are you sure you're okay, Hay?" Caroline set down her toothbrush and cocked her head to the side at Hayley, "You kept asking that sort of thing last night, too."

"I know I did," Hayley let out an embarrassed breath, "So, did you see anything?"

"Again, no I didn't. You were very flustered when I came back outside. You didn't tell me why you were, you just left to go to bed. What's going on? Why won't you tell me?"

"I can't because I don't know what the deal is. I've just felt so weird for a few days."

"Do you think you're sick?" Caroline questioned.

"I don't feel sick. I feel like I'm losing my mind. I've had nothing but nightmares since I started feeling like this. That's why I couldn't sleep."

"Nightmares? What kind of nightmares?"

"Awful ones. Full of horrible things like I've never seen. I don't even know what they are. They seem like demons or monsters or something."

Caroline let a small chuckle slip. "Monsters? Really?"

"Oh, shut up," brushing off Caroline's subtle barb, "Not monsters like little kids are afraid of. Like disfigured people crawling from the walls."

"Ah, I see how that could be a bit unnerving," Caroline furrowed her brow, "have you been watching scary movies or something?"

"Seriously? You know I don't like movies like that," Hayley laughed, "plus, normal nightmares aren't anything like these."

"What do you mean like these?" Caroline picked up her hairbrush as she continued searching for answers. Her concern for her sister began growing as Hayley explained her dreams.

"The room smelled like smoke when I snapped out of it. How? Everything just disappeared," Hayley lifted her hand and snapped her fingers, "just like that. The strangest thing is that I am almost certain that I wasn't asleep when any of this happened."

"Wait, what? You were having a nightmare while you were awake? How?"

"I don't know, Care. I have no idea how to describe it. It was so strange that I feel like it had to be a dream, but so real and I know I fell asleep later because I was up for so long after," shrugging her shoulders and flipping her hands in frustration, "I don't think I've ever hallucinated before so I can't say for certain that's what it was, but if it wasn't then I've got no earthly idea what the heck it was."

Caroline brushed her hair in silence for a moment before setting the brush down on the counter and looked at her sister. "Don't get mad when I ask this, but are you on something?"

"Really, Care? You think I'm on drugs?!" Hayley snapped.

"No, I was just trying to eliminate possible causes, I promise. I know you're not like that."

Hayley shook her head, "At this point, I wish I was on drugs. It would a lot easier to see why I feel like a crazy person. I could definitely do without ever having this stuff happen again, though, I'll tell you that much."

"You should probably take it easy today. Try not to get yourself all worked up at school," Caroline set her brush back in the cabinet and tossed her hair back, "I have to finish getting ready. You sure you're ok?"

Hayley sarcastically laughed at the question, "No, but I'm sure I'll manage somehow. I always do," her voice began to shake as she answered. Her vision began to blur as tears welled in her eyes.

"I know. You're a tough one to crack," Caroline smiled and grabbed Hayley's shoulder as she passed, "I'll be downstairs when you're ready."

Hayley heard the soft click of Caroline's door and closed the door to the bathroom. Taking a deep breath through her nose she lifted her eyes to the mirror. Hayley's face was framed by a small bit of steam that lingered on the bathroom mirror from the shower. A tear rolled down her cheek and past her lips. She suppressed a sob as her lips began to shake. Her fist tightened and tightened until her knuckles turned white. Another sob rose in her throat and forced its way out. Hayley closed the toilet lid and sat down as she began to cry. Her fear and frustration from her hallucination and insomnia had broken and boiled over.

With a swift pound of her fist on the counter, her tears quickly subsided. *No. Not anymore. I'm done being weak. I'm a fighter.* No longer did she feel like the quiet mouse in the corner. Her timid heart had been replaced with the heart of a lion. She wiped away the wet stripes on her cheeks and looked at herself in the mirror once more. This time she did not see the girl who let people walk over her and push her around. She saw someone new. The girl in the mirror stood with such confidence and pride. Fear was not a part of her as it was before. Her eyes carried a powerful darkness and strength. A girl covered in armor, impenetrable shields from the world around her. Her eyebrow rose at the sight of this new Hayley. A burning desire grew in her chest. Things were going to change starting right now. The corners of her mouth curled into a confident smirk as she pulled herself away from the mirror.

"Hayley, come and eat before you go," Amy called out from the kitchen.

"Be there in a minute."

Hayley worked up a small layer of make-up to cover up her obvious exhaustion the best she could and left the bathroom. On her way down the hall to the stairs she kept a steady gaze on the floor a few feet in front of her as if she was building power inside her heart to face the day. One deep breath after another. One step after another. Determination flowed through her veins like rapids. Her days as a pushover were done. She was not ready to allow her daily fate to overcome this new fire. Her first step sat below her, mere steps away. Her family. A sanctuary and a warzone divided by the finest of lines. One false step and she would be slammed back into her normal routine.

Hayley came into the kitchen in her favorite black shirt and red jeans. Both Caroline and her mother lifted their heads and greeted with small smiles as Hayley walked to her seat. Amy looked over to Hayley as she set her fork down. "Feeling okay today, sweetie?"

Hayley held back a laugh at what appeared to be a repeat of her previous conversation with Caroline, "Not really. Totally exhausted."

"Why? You went to bed so early last night."

"I didn't sleep at all last night. I was up all night trying to and finally drifted off around five o'clock."

"Why couldn't you sleep?" Amy prodded.

"I don't know, Mom," Hayley said with frustration, "I'd rather not talk about it, though."

Amy uncomfortably poked at her breakfast, unsure what to say next. Caroline jumped in to help her sister a bit, "She's been having extra stress at school lately. I think that's causing her to lose sleep."

"Yeah, it, uh, must be that," Hayley agreed, nodding her head to Caroline. She knew that Caroline knew there were not any new additional stressors at school. Her sister stepped in simply to pull attention away the truth.

"Oh really? What's going on?" Amy's expression grew more suspiciously inquisitive.

Hayley made up a phony excuse to answer the question, "Just getting all of my work and projects done on time. It can get pretty stressful at times."

"So what's really going on, Hayley?" Amy dropped her hands onto the table, "I know you handle all of your work just fine. You always have." She was not falling for the girls' charade.

"I've just been feeling," Hayley paused and shook her head in confusion, "very weird lately, Mom. I don't want to talk about it."

"Weird how? What's wrong?"

"I don't know! Just let it go!" Hayley slammed her hands down on the table and stormed out of the room.

Amy called out to Hayley as she slammed the door. "I don't know what to do about that," Amy dropped her head toward her plate, "How do I get her to open up to me like she used to?"

"Just forget about it, Mom. She's just had a really hard time sleeping lately, I think it's just made her very cranky," Caroline continued trying to calm her mother, "She told me she has had some very bad nightmares the last couple nights and hasn't been able to sleep well."

"That's no reason to storm out like a child."

"I know, Mom, but just let her go and cool off. I'm sure she'll be fine after a while. She was really frazzled when she came into the bathroom this morning to get ready. Her hair was sticking out every which way," Caroline whirled her hands around her head, "and she looked like a zombie when she walked in." Caroline giggled slightly at the thought of her sister as a zombie before Amy cut in again.

"I understand she was out with a boy a while back. She's not sneaking out to go see him at night is she?" Amy's accusatory tone struck a nerve with Caroline.

"Mother, please, do you really think that Hayley of all people would sneak out just to go see a boy? She's never done anything like that in her life. I don't think that's going to start now."

"Will you at least try to keep tabs on her today? I don't want anything to happen just because she's upset at me."

"I will, Mom. She's not upset at you, though. She's just wiped out and cranky. I'll try and keep a look out for her, even though I don't see her much at school, and help however I can." Caroline grabbed her and Hayley's plates from the table and scraped the half eaten meal off her sister's plate and set the dishes by the sink.

"Thank you, sweetheart. Have a good day." Amy waved as Caroline walked out the front door to meet Hayley at the car.

The humidity was stifling this day. A simple trip outside felt like wading through a swamp. Hayley waited outside and was leaning against the driver side door when Caroline arrived. Hayley let out a frustrated breath, "About time. You ready to go yet?"

"Yes, sorry," Caroline said, annoyed at her sister's attitude, "Mom was just talking to me. Let's go."

Hayley slammed the door behind her as she got into the car. The short drive to school was filled with a tense silence. Caroline had had enough of Hayley's attitude already so she kept her thoughts to herself for the ride's duration. Hayley could be heard mumbling to herself as she turned down the lane of the parking lot. Caroline could only hear one word above the quiet muttering. Hate.

"What do you hate, Hay?"

"What do I hate? I hate her," Hayley thrust her arm forward pointing to a large, dark haired girl sitting on the bed of a pickup truck in the lot, "I hate Beth. She is the one that causes all of my problems. She is a demon. I would give almost anything to just punch her as hard as I can in the mouth."

"Hayley! Don't say that, that's awful."

"She's awful. I'm done taking her crap every day."

"So don't let her bother you. You definitely don't need to fight her though. That will just cause more problems."

Hayley parked the car and opened her door, "I'm not going to fight her. Not yet at least. I'm no fortune teller, though. I can't make any guarantees for the future."

The burning in Hayley's chest grew stronger when she looked at Beth again. She kept her eyes glued on Beth's as she grabbed her bag from the car. Her gaze did not move from Beth's eyes as she closed the gap between them. As she got closer Beth shifted her eyes to Hayley and saw her staring at her.

"What the hell are you looking at?" Beth barked. Her ebony hair bounced when she snapped her words out. Hayley continued walking in silence, yet kept her eyes dead set on her enemy. "Hey! I said, what are you looking at, moron?" Beth shouted again, trying to gain Hayley's attention. Hayley's eyes narrowed as she raised one eyebrow toward Beth. A defiant smirk curled in the corners of Hayley's lips. Beth's anger was very apparent now. "You're making a big mistake, Audige. You know you are."

Hayley continued past Beth and into the building. Her eyes narrowed as her smirk grew into a defiant smile. Beth did not know how to handle her personal whipping post turning against her. Caroline following close behind Hayley, shocked at what she just witnessed. Her sister seemed more like a complete stranger now. The Hayley she knew would never throw sparks like that.

"What was that all about?" Caroline questioned.

"I told you. I'm done with her. It ends today."

= *11* =

Devin stood at his locker as Hayley turned into the hallway near the front door of the school. He turned to find Hayley quickly walking towards him. He turned away from his locker to speak to her.

"Hey there," Devin leaned against his locker and smiled, "how was y-"

"I hate her," Hayley snapped.

"Whoa, whoa, whoa, hate who, what's going on?" Devin replied, shocked at Hayley's unusually harsh attitude this morning.

"Beth. I hate her. I have done nothing to make her act like she does to me."

"Oh, yeah, that's just Beth, Hayley. She's just a mean person. Try not to let her get in your head. That's her game."

"Well, it's too late for that," Hayley shook her head, "She already has been and I'm done with her. I'm going to make it stop."

"How do you exactly plan on doing that?" Devin questioned.

Hayley paused and shrugged her shoulders. Her train of thought on the matter had yet to deliver a concrete answer to the issue. "I don't know yet. I'll figure it out, though. It ends today, I know that much."

Devin grabbed Hayley's arm, "Don't do anything crazy, okay? You know what happened when I let my emotions get the best of me."

"I know, Devin. I can't make any guarantees about anything, though. If she pushes me today, it's coming back tenfold."

"I really don't like how that sounds, Hayley."

"It needs to be done. She needs to know that she is not above anyone."

"I agree that she needs to know that, but I don't think fighting or anything harsh is going to prove that. She has to know that she's not as smart as you and I'm sure that bothers her to no end."

"I don't care what she knows, I-"

"Just don't do anything stupid, okay?" Devin interrupted, placing his hand on Hayley's shoulder, "I know you're better than that."

With a simple nod Hayley turned away from Devin. She walked to her locker mumbling to herself about Beth. The swarms of kids around her seemed to disappear from her mind as she focused on ending her torturous time at Theroux. Hayley pulled her locker door open and looked over the books and papers inside. Her blank stare left her dead to the world while her brain churned. Plans of how to finally strike back at her oppressors flooded her mind. *Fight. Fight. Fight.* A simple answer always came through. A simple answer but far from a simple plan. A physical altercation was not going to do any good. It never would. Only proving she was no longer scared would leave the impression she needed.

The slam of a nearby locker snapped Hayley back to reality. She shook her head and placed her books from her backpack inside her locker. Her hand slid off the books' spines and revealed the worn leather binding of the mysterious old notebook. Hayley stared at the old book in shock. She had no recollection of ever putting the notebook in her bag at all. *How did this end up in my bag?*

Hayley's locker door swung farther open. She kept her eyes glued to the notebook, unable to divert her stare. Jeff, her locker neighbor for all of high school stood alternating his gaze from Hayley to her locker and back again. His eyebrows lifted from his confusion.

"Still on Earth there, Hayley?" Jeff joked.

"What?" Hayley snapped back into focus, "Oh, yeah. I'm... I'm fine."

"What the heck are you staring at?"

"This," Hayley pulled the old notebook from the pile of books and turned it to Jeff, "I got it at a garage sale."

"So, what is it?" Jeff questioned, "Just a book?"

Hayley put the book back onto the pile, "It's actually a notebook. I don't have any idea how it ended up in my bag, though. The last thing I remember doing was leaving it my bedroom."

"Oh, you probably just grabbed it without thinking about it."

"I must have. I don't see any other way it could have gotten here otherwise."

"Could have always been a goblin too, or a leprechaun," Jeff laughed.

"I guess that's always a possibility," Hayley chuckled, playing along, "we'll go ahead and say it was one of those."

"I'll see you later, Hayley." Jeff turned around and left for class, leaving Hayley at her locker.

Hayley looked around the hallway before looking back to the notebook. She pulled it off of the stack of books and examined the front cover. The leather felt warm in her hands, like it was becoming part of her. The hallway light revealed dust covering the stone. Hayley slid her thumb over the gem, leaving a small clean line across its diameter. A small shadow moved across the stone, disappearing into the dust on the side. Hayley's eyes narrowed as she tried to find the shadow inside the stone. She used the hem of her shirt and wiped away the remaining dust.

Turning the book under the light she looked for the shadow once more. The opaque stone appeared to become more transparent the longer Hayley looked into it. Just before she lifted her head from the book, the shadow darted across the stone once again catching her attention. Its intermittent motions began to quicken until the small shadow began to swirl in the black pool. The shadow grew and grew until it filled the entire stone. A faint orange glow appeared in the center of the shadow like a distant flame. Dark smoke seeped from the edges of the stone and rose through the air. The black gas lifted straight into Hayley's face. Her sudden gasp caused her to breathe in the ebony smoke. Panic quickly set in as she choked on the gas. As quickly as her coughing attack came, it subsided. Hayley stood with her head down, bracing herself on her locker.

Hayley's violent coughs caught the attention of the other students around her. A short brown haired girl came to Hayley's side.

"Are you okay?" The girl asked.

"Get away from me!" Hayley yelled, her voice dark, raspy, and strained. Inhuman.

"What's wrong with you?" The other girl asked, shocked at the tone she just received.

"Leave. Now!" Hayley quickly shot her glance to the girl. Her eyes glossed over and darkening as if they were being filled with the smoke she inhaled. The girl quickly jumped back, her eyes wide open and hand over her mouth. She turned and ran from Hayley.

The bell sounded and Hayley shook herself back to reality. She closed her eyes and rubbed them roughly, trying to clear her vision. The darkness in her eyes slowly lifted. Once her sight returned to normal, she gathered her books as if nothing happened. The hallway was oddly silent for being so full. Hayley quickly realized that the majority of the students near her were staring at her with shocked looks on their faces. Her loud exchange with the small girl caught the attention of nearly everyone around. Embarrassed, she lowered her head and made her way to class. Her first steps felt like walking in quicksand, something was pulling her back to her locker. She was, however, able to drown out the feeling and get to her class.

Students milled about the room as she entered and worked through them to her seat. Hayley sat quietly with her head drooped toward her desktop. A horrible headache soon swelled inside of her. She placed both hands on her temples and massaged her head, trying to rid herself of the pain. The circular motions only seemed to push the pain deeper. The rubbing of her hands felt like two grindstones pulverizing her skull. The bright lights in the room only worsened her already dwindling condition. Lifting her head toward the front of the room, Hayley saw that her teacher had already begun the lesson. She did not hear her begin speaking at all. Soon Hayley's breathing began to quicken and her vision blurred. Her hand shot in the air for her teacher's attention.

"Yes, Hayley?"

"May I be excused? I think I might be sick," Hayley pleaded, "really soon."

"Of course, please go." Her teacher gestured to the door and Hayley dashed out, bumping her hip firmly into the desk nearest to the door causing quiet giggles and snickers to fill the room. She took a few quick steps down the hallway from the classroom door before slowing to a walk. Her face had been drained off all of its color. Her vision had cleared slightly since she was sitting. Halfway down the hallway Hayley's eyes fixed on her locker. As if something inside of it was calling out to her, pulling her closer, forcing her to move nearer.

She stumbled over her feet and braced herself against the wall of lockers to her left. Her vision shuddered and she stumbled again. The lines of grout in the tile floor began to blur and disappear as her vision got darker. She lifted her head toward her locker and saw smoke coming from inside. She clumsily rushed to the door and took her lock off. When she opened the door, a wall of black smoke poured out from inside. Hayley gasped and jumped back. She grasped the door for stability. The smoke overwhelmed her, her eyes rolled back in her head and she collapsed forward to the floor. Her head hit the hinge of the locker next to hers. Her body slammed to the floor with a resounding thud.

A burning glow broke out in the darkness like a distant fire. The sound of heavy breathing grew more and more audible. The glowing light began to be broken by a slowly appearing object. The dark object grew and shifted in size as it appeared. Fingers sprouted from the ambiguous object. The long fingers, dry and bloody, cracked as they shifted. The hand turned, curling its finger in a signal to come. Over and over the hand made the signal. The heavy breathing grew heavier as the duration of the signals increased.

Hayley opened her eyes to find herself in a closed dark room The light of the adjacent room shined through the window in the door. She recognized the front office of the school as the other room. She rose off her back alone on the small couch. A single clock could be heard ticking on the wall. *How long have I been in here?* The sound of footsteps could be heard getting closer and closer. Hayley's nerves tensed as she prepared for someone to come inside. The shadow of unknown feet appeared under the door. Hayley watched the door knob turn and open the door. The school nurse peeked her head in the room and turned on the lights. Hayley quickly relaxed from her tense position while squinting her eyes from the light.

"Oh good, you're awake," Mrs. Bell happily exclaimed, "How are you doing, Hayley?"

"I'm okay, I think. My head doesn't hurt so much now," Hayley lifted her hand to massage the back of her own neck, "Do you know what happened?"

"We're not entirely sure. We heard a crash in the hall and found you lying next to your locker. I think it looks like your fall was nastier than it really was. You've got a cut on your forehead. We've been checking on you every few minutes to make sure you were alright."

"I don't remember falling. I remember feeling very sick and leaving class. Everything kind of blurs after that and then I woke up."

"It seems like you just fainted," Mrs. Bell handed Hayley a glass of water, "Just relax here for now. You don't seem to be injured apart from the cut and a couple bumps on your arm, so once you're alright you can go on with your day. Unless, that is, you feel you need to go home. In that case just let me know and we'll call your mom."

"I think I'll be okay. I'll probably just stay. I have stuff to do anyway."

"Alright, just let me know before you go back. Be careful out there."

"I will. Thanks, Mrs. Bell."

Mrs. Bell closed the door behind her as she left her office. Hayley sat on the couch for a few minutes to collect her thoughts. The cut on her head stung when she touched it. Upon further inspection in the mirror, the cut was not very deep and could easily be hidden by her hair. Hayley moved into the bathroom attached to the office and splashed some cold water on her face. The cool water helped soothe her mind and cut. Rubbing her wet hands over her eyes, she could breathe a bit easier and more relaxed. She dried her face, grabbed her bag, and left the nurse's office.

"I'm leaving now, Mrs. Bell"

"Okay, Hayley," Mrs. Bell waved from across the main office, "feel better."

Hayley meandered through the main office door and back toward her class. The hallways were much louder than normal. She turned and looked back at the clock in the office, nearly falling over in shock when she saw what the time. 11:52. *Two and half hours! I've been gone for two and a half hours?* Lunch was nearly upon her already. *Maybe some food will fix my mind.* A couple minutes after leaving the office, the bell sounded and students flooded the hallway to head to lunch. Hayley dipped and turned her way through the masses toward the lunch room.

Her quick paces were brought to a halt when the grinding in her mind came back. Placing one hand against her temple, she squeezed her eyes shut as tight as she could. The pain drilling into her head like it had during class. Her body tensed and she clenched her fist. Pain giving way to anger. The more it hurt, the angrier she became. A new feeling emerged inside of her. A sudden pulling on her mind. She quickly changed her direction and headed for her locker instead of the cafeteria.

= 12 =

Her agile walk from moments early had now been replaced by a determined powerful march. She refused to move for anyone, simply walking through and pushing anyone that got in her way. Complaints of those being forcibly moved fell upon deaf ears as she continued through the hallway.

I have to get back, I must. Why? Her thoughts were eliminated and swapped with one solitary desire. She needed to get back to her locker. Something was calling her back. *Why?* The crowded hallway quickly dwindled down to a few stragglers here and there. Hayley arrived at her locker and stared straight at it, not moving an inch. She placed her hand on the cool metal door. An unknown warmth shot through Hayley's hand and continued through her body. In a flash her mind went blank. She opened her locker and immediately grabbed the old notebook.

Now more than ever the book felt like a part of her. She felt as though it was connected directly to her mind.

The leather cover gave off a strange slight pulsing sensation to Hayley's hands, like a heartbeat. She inspected the gem in the cover. The shadow from earlier in the morning was gone, however, she could still see something inside the stone. Hayley pulled the book closer to her face to peer into the black stone. Inside the stone a dark silhouetted figure could be seen. The figure was motionless until it opened its eyes. Two glowing orange eyes burned from under its eyelids. The dim warm glow revealed the creatures teeth, jagged and razor sharp. It's skin appeared cracked and decaying in the faint light. The embers vanished as quickly as they had appeared, and the creature was gone. The stone faded back to its original dull dusty shimmer.

The aggressive clawing in Hayley's mind, momentarily sidetracked by what had just occurred, continued to drag her thoughts back to the locker. She lifted her head and looked around the hallway to see that she was the only one in sight. Undeniable now, thoughts of the book ripped her mind back into its focus. Opening the book she found another mysterious passage.

Embers burn in the hearts of the stricken

Souls tattered and torn

Beaten, blood left to thicken

Storms of rage are born

Where are these things coming from? Her mind grew even more confused. Hayley's brow wrinkled at the cryptic message. This message appeared to make less sense than the first. Frustrated, Hayley ripped the page out of the book and shoved it into her pocket. Her locker door slammed shut as she stormed away. With the loud crash, her mind cleared and she regained her focus. Her insatiable desire to be at her locker disappeared as quickly as it arose. The hallway began to clear out as most of the students made their way to lunch. Sounds of footsteps faded from earshot.

Quiet clinks of metal sounded as Hayley dragged her fingers along the lockers. Her gaze was uninterrupted as she marched through the now empty hallway, her pace constant. Hayley's fingers fell away from the lockers as she reached a doorway, room 102, the science lab. She walked past the door without a thought but stopped shortly after and glanced back. The itching in her head began to return, pulling her to the door. She looked through the window of the door and saw that the room was dark and empty. With two quick glances, checking for any other people, she entered the empty science lab.

Beakers, instruments, and books lined the tables and shelves of the room. Hayley did not turn on the lights as there was enough natural light coming in through the windows to see sufficiently. She quietly walked over to a lab table that was out of sight from the hallway. Hayley pulled the crinkled passage from her pocket and placed it in front of herself. Its words stared into her soul as she attempted to figure it out again. *What does this m--- No. I don't care anymore.* The frustration in her mind had reached its end. Her eyes wandered from the page to the Bunsen Burner on the table and back to the torn and wrinkled page. A small smirk grew from her lips.

Thinking back to her experience at the fire pit, she wondered if this page would burn with the same intensity as the last.

Let's find out.

All of the pieces to the burner were directly in front of her on the table. She quickly assembled the apparatus as she had many times before. Careful to keep everything quiet, every movement and action was slow and deliberate. Hayley firmly grasped the gas valve. She began to turn the gas on but quickly shut it off again. Her mind shifted and she began having second thoughts about burning the page in such a risky place. The room remained as silent as it had been the whole time. Hayley remained alone in the room. She slipped over to the door and peeked out of its window. No one was around. Lunch had already begun. Students in class had already reached their rooms. The hallway was silent and empty.

Hayley turned her back to the door and walked back to the table with the prepared burner. She placed the front of the lighter up to the tip of the burner and turned on the gas. Squeezing the spark lighter, Hayley ignited the burner's flame and picked up the crumpled page. The corner of the page glowed in the firelight. Quickly the corner ignited and began to consume the paper. Its edges began to blacken and fall to ashes. The flames moved faster and faster across the page causing Hayley to drop it from her hand. She quickly ripped her hand away before the flames caught her skin. The page was fully engulfed as it fell to the table. As the page fell the flames began to shift in color as they did at the fire pit. The flames' orange glow faded to blue. The flaming page halted in the air as it fell toward the table. Ashes fell from the page as it burned in front of Hayley. Her satisfaction of burning the page turned to shock as she watched the event unfold. The page began to spin rapidly. Flames spiraled upwards toward the ceiling. With a forceful eruption the page exploded outward, knocking Hayley to the floor.

Beakers and test tubes could be heard shattering around her. The stool she sat on laid next to her head. She crouched down next to the table, trying to hide herself in case somebody heard the disturbance. Hayley sat silently on the floor for a moment and peeked her head out from behind the table. No one could be seen in the room or doorway. Letting out a relieved sigh, she stood back up. Ashes from the explosion were left on the table in a nearly perfect circle. Hayley gave a strong puff and blew the ashes off the table, no one would notice them strewn about the floor with the disaster scene from the shattered equipment. Hayley coughed loudly as some of the ashes floated into her mouth and lungs. Scrambling for a trash can, she swept as much broken glass off of the tables as fast as she could. She quickly gathered herself and suppressed her coughs as she grabbed her bag and darted from the room, leaving the burner on the table and scattered shards of glass on the floor.

Hayley shut the door behind herself and swiftly walked away from the room. Her pace quickened as she felt someone was watching her leave the room. She turned the last corner toward the cafeteria and ran into Mrs. Florence as she also came around the corner.

"Oh," Hayley grunted, "Sorry Mrs. F."

"It's okay, Hayley, what are you still doing out here? You know it's time for lunch."

"Yeah, I, um," Hayley's voice shook, "forgot something in my locker. I'm going right now."

"Did you notice anything strange back there? Like a loud crash or anything?"

"No, I didn't notice anything. Why what happened?"

"Well, I was told there was a loud noise that came from somewhere around the classrooms over there and was on my way to check it out."

"No I didn't notice anything. Sorry."

"Ok. Thanks, Hayley."

Hayley darted away to the lunch room as quickly as she could. The cafeteria line moved as slowly as usual. Smells of fresh fries and pizza filled the air. The cafeteria was always much hotter than the rest of the school due to its abundance of windows. The combination of late Louisiana spring heat and a room full of people made for a sweltering, sticky room. Tempers had flared up once or twice this year from escalating small arguments. Staff often placed the blame of the behavior on the heat rather than the parties of the fight. Stating that it makes everyone a little crazy to be in that heat every day.

Hayley took her food from the line and made her way across the floor to the empty table near the side exit of the building. As she twisted and turned around the people, chairs, and tables in the room, Beth rose from her seat. She pushed her seat aside and took three large steps to put herself in Hayley's path. Her snaggletooth grin sat at Hayley's eye level. Hayley moved slightly to one side to subtly try to avoid conflict.

"Where do you think you're going?" Beth asked, again moving in front of Hayley, "You know you really messed up this morning with your attitude to me."

"Get out of my way, Beth." Hayley calmly demanded.

"Why? What the hell do you honestly think you could even do to me?"

"Just move. I don't have time to deal with idiots today."

"Excuse me?!" Beth exclaimed, "Who do you think you're talking to like that?" Beth shot her hand forward and pushed Hayley's shoulder.

Hayley took a deep breath before responding. "Get out of my way." Hayley slowly said through gritted teeth, her anger growing with every passing second.

"Or what? You gonna rat me out to the principal? Like I give a rat's ass what he thinks."

"Move. Now." Hayley quietly demanded.

"Not gonna happen," Beth chuckled and paused, "You know what? I think it's time I really taught you a lesson." She reached out and shoved Hayley's shoulder once again. "Just like I thought. Once a weakling, always a weakling. You really must hate yourself, bitch." With one strong swing, Beth pushed Hayley's lunch tray back into her chest. Hayley gasped as the tray hit her. The pizza slice and basket of fries smashed into Hayley's shirt, leaving a large greasy stain on her shirt as they slid toward the floor.

A crowd of students began to surround the two girls. Shouts of "Fight! Fight!" could be heard from different sides of the swarm. Hayley looked down at the mess on her clothes and slowly lifted her head back to Beth. She stood opposite Hayley with a cocky, pleased smirk on her face. Hayley's eyes widened as she planted her feet solidly on the floor and shoved Beth with both hands. Beth took one large step backwards before catching herself. Hayley's anger boiled inside of her. Beth, now livid, quickly got back into Hayley's face.

"What the hell is wrong with you?" Beth yelled, "Are you trying to get your ass kicked?"

A fire exploded in Hayley's chest as she stood straight up directly in front of Beth's face. "Try me." As soon as those two simple words were spoken, Hayley's vision began to blur. The loud shouts of the crowd began to fade away to a drowning silence.

The room appeared to get darker as she grew angrier . Her anger had taken over. The color faded from her eyes as they began to blacken like the stone of the book. Her mind went black and she turned her shoulder to throw a punch at Beth when a hand grabbed on to her shoulder. The person who grabbed Hayley meant business, as the grasp did not let up at all. Their fingertips pressing firmly into her shoulder.

Devin pulled the girls apart and brought Hayley away from Beth. "What the heck are you doing? Knock it off!" His angry face quickly turned to shock when he looked into her eyes. The crowd around the girls began to dissipate as the tension had been quelled.

Hayley remained silent as she stared lifelessly through Devin. Her rage coursing through her veins. Deep growl-like rumblings could be heard coming from Hayley's throat. Hands trembling, joints locked, and teeth grinding, she had lost all contact with reality. She twisted her shoulders to try and break free of his grasp. With each violent movement, she struggled to release herself but Devin was too strong to defeat. He shook her shoulders as he tried to snap her out of this state. "Hayley! Look at me!" He shouted, "Pay attention!"

Devin grabbed Hayley's forearm and pulled her aside. He returned his sight to Beth, still standing across from Hayley with her arms folded defiantly. Pointing directly into Beth's face he demanded, "Knock it off, all of it. She's never done anything to you. Grow up."

"She nothing but a little b--"

"Shut up!" Devin strongly interrupted, "I don't want to hear it anymore. You understand me?" He walked Hayley into the hallway outside of the cafeteria. Hayley froze. The tension in her body began to loosen. Her shoulders relaxed and she stared straight ahead again. The black slowly began to drain from her eyes as her mind regained its focus. Her jaw dropped as if she had lost all of her strength to hold it.

"Hayley, are you with me?" He asked.

With a grunting sigh Hayley was able to speak, "What, Devin? What?"

"Why in the world are you trying to fight Beth?"

"What? What are you talking about?" Hayley questioned, "I never did that."

"Seriously? You just did it no more than two minutes ago. What are you thinking trying to fight her? That's not like you at all."

"I don't know what you're talking about, Devin. I don't remember anything like that ever happening," she grabbed the sides of her head, "Ugh, my head is killing me. I feel like something just ripped out of my skull."

"Are you sure you're okay? Devin lowered his hands, "I heard about what happened earlier. You need to get out of here and rest. Something is obviously not right." He looked at the large stain on her shirt, "That's a nasty stain you've got there. I've got an extra shirt in my locker if you want it."

Hayley pulled away from Devin, "No, I'll be fine. Thanks, though. Please just let me be, I don't need help."

"You do need help. Something is wrong. People don't just black out for no reason, Hayley. Do you remember anything about what I told you at Josiah's?" Devin shook his head, "Please do not make the same mistakes I made. She wins if you snap, do you realize that?"

"I don't--" Hayley paused and looked at the ground, a lump rose in her throat, "I don't need anyone's help. Just let me be, please. I'll be alright."

"Fine, be careful trying to be a one man army. Constantly denying help only will push people away," Devin stepped back and pointed at Hayley, "but I know everything isn't okay and you know it, too. Please, just promise me that you'll be careful."

Hayley silently turned and walked away shaking her head. Her headache growing in intensity. The hallway seemed to go on forever as she slowly walked back toward her locker. It became increasingly difficult to focus on anything but the burning, pulling feeling in her mind. Her mind wandered more and more as her grip on reality felt to be slipping with each step she took.

= 13 =

Lunch was over and classes had begun again. The quiet of the classrooms was broken by school PA system. "Hayley Audige, please report to the main office." Hayley's stomach sank. She had never been called to the office for discipline before. The entire class turned and looked in shock at Hayley, knowing her normal timid nature. She dropped her head, gathered her things, and slowly rose out of her seat. The short walk to the principal's office felt like miles. Her mind filled with every possible scenario that could play out in her meeting with the principal.

She slowly walked into the front office and took her seat outside of the principal's office. Her headache still pounding. The principal, Mr. Johnstone, opened his door and poked his head out, "You can come in now, Hayley."

Hayley, visibly nervous, took her seat inside his office and kept her gaze away from his eyes.

"I assume you know why you're here, Hayley," Mr. Johnstone said, hands folded on his desk, "Tell me what happened. I have Beth coming in here once we're finished to tell her side."

"I'm sorry for what happened," Hayley sighed, "but she bothers me and picks on me on a daily basis. Pushing me, bullying me, and calling me names. I just had had enough and pushed back, but that was all that happened, honestly, I only pushed her once before Devin pulled us apart."

Mr. Johnstone let out a small breath, "Look, I know Beth's reputation around the school, and I know yours. You're not a bad kid."

"I didn't mean for any-"

"I know, Hayley," the principal interrupted, "I know you didn't mean for it escalate like it did, but you know that we can't have things like that happening in the school."

Hayley dropped her head again and quietly said, "I know, I'm sorry."

"Since there was no real fight or punches thrown, I am going to let you off with a warning. Just so you know, Beth will also be let off with only a warning."

"Thank you so much. I promise it won't happen again." Hayley felt a huge weight come off of her shoulders as she avoided any punishment.

"See that it doesn't. I promise I won't be so lenient next time," Mr. Johnstone signaled to the door, "Now get back to class."

The bell sounded as Hayley walked out of his office. She gathered her belongings and walked to her next class. The rest of the afternoon passed without any further incidents. The final school bell sounded like a reprieve to Hayley. She drove Caroline home as she did every day since she learned to drive. She refused to let Caroline drive despite her dwindling condition throughout the day. Caroline's pleas to her sister went unanswered. Her horrible headache still lingered from the earlier cafeteria confrontation with Beth. The afternoon sun hurt her eyes and exacerbated her pain. Her dark sunglasses did nothing to help quell its sting.

"Hayley, what's wrong?" Caroline questioned, "Why are you in such a bad mood?"

Hayley sighed, "I don't want to talk about it, Care."

"Tell me. Is it because of what happened with Beth?"

"What?" Hayley looked to her sister, "How do you know about that?"

"Seriously, Hay? People home sick today already know. What happened?"

Hayley pulled onto her street and proceeded to confess what happened earlier that day. "She just finally went too far. I couldn't stop myself. I wanted to teach her that she can't just walk all over me anymore."

"I know, but you didn't actually try to fight her did you?"

"No. Devin stepped in before anything got out of hand. That didn't stop everyone from getting loud and causing a scene, though." Hayley let out a quick puff of breath, "Why does everyone think that I wouldn't be able to hold my own against her?"

"Hayley, she's almost twice your size."

"I don't care how big that troll is. She's not something I'm afraid of anymore."

"I just don't want you to get into any trouble."

"I will be just fine," Hayley's frustration began to boil over, "I don't need your help, okay?"

"Fine. Whatever." Caroline quietly looked out the window and watched as they approached their house, unsatisfied with how her conversation with her sister abruptly ended. Hayley pulled into the driveway and shut the car off. She grabbed her bag, slammed the door behind herself and walked into the house. Caroline shook her head at her sister's attitude and followed inside. She couldn't help but wonder what had become of her sister.

Hayley left the door open when she entered the house. With a frustrated huff she took her shoes off and immediately climbed the stairs to her room. She threw her bag on the floor and fell onto her bed. The sunlight outside hurt Hayley's eyes and continued to aggravate her already painful headache. She reached out toward her window, grabbed the curtains and closed them. The shade cooled the room and relieved her eye pain. She lay on her bed, breathing deeply, staring at the ceiling, and focusing on the silence.

Her frustrations began to diminish as she grew more relaxed and sleepy. Turning onto her side, she closed her eyes and drifted into a shallow sleep.

The bedroom became illuminated with a harsh white light. Hayley awoke on the cold floor. She squinted as the light made it difficult to see. Two figures could be seen sitting across from her in the room. Everything in the room was blurred in the bright light. As her vision cleared, she glanced around the room. The shape of the room hinted that it was her own bedroom, yet nothing remained of the room she knew. The room was empty. The walls were empty. The floor was stark white, as was the ceiling. The windowless walls gave no sense of relief from the anxiety brewing in Hayley's mind. The deep thumping of a heartbeat shook in the walls. The rhythmic pounding grew faster as Hayley became more and more nervous. She continued scanning the room until the shaking of chains interrupted her focus. She had forgotten about the two figures across from her.

Hayley looked to the bodies in front of her. Each appeared to be feminine, one blonde and one with hair of auburn. They sat with their heads pointed to the floor. The arms of each were chained to the floor. The heavy iron chain links scraped along the floor as they shifted their arms. One girl breathed heavily while the other could be heard weeping. Their hair hung dirty and rustled off of their heads. The white cloth robes wrapping their bodies were tattered, dirty, and burned. The arms of each person were burned and bruised to the point that any spot of a healthy flesh tone was difficult to find. The skin was dry and cracked. Dried blood was smeared on the wrists of the blonde girl on the left, wounds marked the length of her forearms. Her deep sobs could easily be heard across the room. Her misery was blazingly evident.

Hayley, growing more and more panicked, scooted backwards until she bumped into the wall. The sliding of her feet alerted the two girls and they slowly raised their heads. Hayley quickly recognized the features of each girl as those of her own and Caroline. Their faces as mangled as their arms. The faces of the girls were disfigured with harsh burns. Their eyes, darker than midnight, appeared like black holes in their faces. Hayley's heart raced with fear. Her voice sat paralyzed in her throat. The ever-present ghostly heartbeat grew faster as her fear rose. Unable to scream she sat horrified and watched as they struggled in their chains. The disfigured Hayley pulled and pulled at her chains attempting to free herself. Hayley gathered herself enough to shake out a simple question, "Who... who did this to you?"

The tortured Hayley stopped pulling at her chains and sat still. She stared directly into her counterparts eyes and slowly lifted her hand and pointed at Hayley. The cracked and broken hand felt like an arrow through her heart. Hayley sat stunned at this revelation as tears burned in her eyes. She choked out a broken plea to the mangled girls, "How? I... couldn't..." Her tears now rolled down her face as she fell into despair, "I'm so sorry." The dark Hayley's breathing grew more intense as her face twisted in anger. She thrust her arm forward, snapping one chain from the floor, growling in fury. Flames erupted outward from under the broken clasp on the floor, igniting the ivory flooring into a slowly growing fire. Hayley jumped to her feet and began to search for a way out of the room.

Her evil doppelganger snarled and struggled to snap the remaining chain as the floor burned around her. Hayley's nails scratched and slid across the smooth white walls. Hayley pounded on the walls in a panic for her own life. The fire grew around the two girls on the floor. The disfigured Caroline continued to sob as she examined her wounds and burns. The bloodied Hayley gave a final powerful twist of the chain. The chain shattered with a great snap. Metal shards bounced off the floor in all directions. Hayley continued to try and find an escape from the room and her attacker, clawing and pounding the wall. She flinched harshly as the shards bounced near her feet. Glancing behind herself she saw that her assailant was now free. Slowly the horrid figure rose to her feet and released a tortured scream. Hayley crumbled in fear as the scream pierced her eardrums. She desperately searched for some semblance of safety in the empty walled prison. Her head dropped and she saw a sharp piece of the thick, broken chain and quickly snatched it off the floor. Her fingers curled around the sharp edges of the metal shard. Its rough sides pressed into her fingers as she raised her hand up toward her shoulder. With all of her power she plunged the shard into the drywall, hopelessly looking for an escape.

Hayley grimaced in pain as the power of her strike forced the sharp edges of the piece of chain dug into her skin. Blood dripped from her fingers down to the floor. She scratched the point of the chain down the wall leaving a deep gash nearly a foot long. Tortured screams came from Caroline's room as she pulled the makeshift blade from the wall. Hayley's heart dropped as she heard the scream. She cried out to her sister, "Caroline! Caroline!" No response could be heard. She screamed her sister's name louder and louder but to no avail. Caroline could not be heard no matter how much Hayley cried out to her. Tears poured from Hayley's eyes as she crumbled to the floor. Her heart broke as she could not come to her little sister's rescue.

Her cheeks burned from her overwhelming fear and sadness. The deep breathing of her doppelganger could be felt on the back of her neck. Hayley's body jolted in shock. She turned to find her enemy inches from her face. Jumping backwards Hayley slammed her head against the wall causing her to lose her footing and fall to the floor. Blurry eyed, she looked up to see her attacker lunge directly at her face. She screamed as she cowered and the room went black.

Shock and the smell of vomit shook Hayley out of her slumber. In a cold sweat, she lifted her head to find herself lying face down on the floor next to her bed. Her head pounded worse than ever. Her hands shook like earthquakes. As she gained her focus, she looked in disgust at the nearly black puddle she left on the floor. The smell nearly drove her to vomit again. Breathing became difficult in between her constant gagging. She braced her hand on the nightstand and pulled herself to her feet. Light still poured through the window over her bed. Hayley's brow furrowed as she gazed in disbelief at the clock. She had only been asleep for half an hour.

How?

= *14* =

"Hayley, come down for dinner," Her mother called up from the kitchen.

Struggling to speak she gave her scratchy response, "I'll be there in a minute, let me wash up real quick." She slowly walked into the bathroom and stared at herself in the mirror. Horribly pale. Paler than she had ever seen herself before. Surely the vomiting was a factor in this. Strangely, the lights around the mirror did not affect her headaches like they had earlier in the day. She ran the water for a moment allowing it to warm. The tepid water relaxed her as she splashed it over her face. Dried vomit lingered on her bottom lip and cheek. She scrubbed her face to clear off the remnants. After patting her face dry she pulled the towel from the rack and brought it back to her room and dropped it over the vomit next to her bed to hide it.

As she turned to walk down the stairs the smell of fresh cooked chicken and vegetables filled her nostrils. A small smile curled in her cheeks from the pleasant aroma yet her stomach still turned. Step by step she walked down to the kitchen. Caroline peered up from her chair and began to give a small grin to her sister. As her lips pulled into a the smile they quickly stopped as she saw how pale her sister appeared. She opened her mouth to ask Hayley what was wrong, but Hayley quickly shook her head and Caroline refrained. Hayley's mother had her back to the girls while she finished preparing dinner.

Amy turned to her two girls, plates in hand, and set them on table. The smell of the meal began to appeal more to Hayley's sensitive stomach. Her attention quickly turned to Hayley's ghostly complexion. "Hayley. Are you alright, sweetheart? I don't think I've ever seen you so pale."

Hayley hesitated, swallowed the lump in her throat, and responded, "I've just been feeling a little off all day. My stomach is just upset right now. No need to worry."

"You don't have to eat if you don't feel well, sweetie."

"I'll be fine. I promise," Hayley gave her mother a small smile and looked back to her food. She poked at the vegetables and moved them around her plate. She fumbled her thoughts around in her mind before finally working up the courage to speak up. "Mom, can I ask you a question?"

"Of course."

"What happened? You know, with you and Dad?"

"What do you mean?" Amy gave her daughter a steely but slightly confused look, "You know what happened, Hayley."

"Yeah, I know what just happened, but things couldn't have always been like that. There's no way things were always that bad. I remember you two being so happy when I was younger," Hayley dropped her head, but kept her eyes on her mother.

"I don't know if I have a solid answer for that. Things just change sometimes. Sometimes small things, and sometimes they're life altering things. This just happened to be one of those things," Amy's voice began to shake, "Sometimes you can do everything right and still be wrong."

"I understand. I'm sorry, Mom." Hayley took several small bites from her dinner before getting up and taking her dishes to the sink.

"Hayley," Her mother called out, "if you're not going to finish that, don't throw it out. I'll put it away and you can finish it tomorrow."

"Alright." Hayley set the dish down on the counter. As soon as the dish touched the stone countertop, a strange pressure took over her stomach. A force pushing out from her abdomen. The pressure grew stronger and stronger as each second passed. Hayley groaned and bent over, placing her hands on her knees. The pressure continued to grow stronger as she stood up again. She glanced down to her stomach and saw underneath her shirt that something was moving. Upon lifting her shirt she discovered something moving underneath her skin, pushing out of her stomach. Hayley gasped and jumped back against the counter.

Unable to make a sound, Hayley stared in terror at the alien object moving inside of her body. One large bulge under her skin divided into five smaller bumps. Her eyes grew larger as she watched this transpire. The small bumps pressed firmer against her stomach and extended outward, four upwards toward her chest and one toward her hip. The pressure grew ever stronger trying to escape her body. The shape of a hand became clear as day as it braced against her skin. Hayley let out a horrified scream at the sight of the foreign object inside of her. Amy and Caroline both jumped out of their seats, knocking over glasses and dropping their silverware.

"Hayley! What's is the matter with you?!" Her mother shouted.

"Help! I don't know what's happening to me!" Hayley cried out, "There's something inside me!"

Amy scrambled over to her daughter and grabbed her shoulders. "What's the matter?" Caroline stood, frightened across the room.

"Look at my stomach, something is moving around in there. Like a hand or something!" Hayley stood quaking as her mother leaned toward her stomach.

"Hayley," Amy said, with a clear sense of annoyance in her voice, "there is *nothing* here, there is nothing inside of you. Relax." She returned to her seat and let out a frustrated huff as she sat down. "Don't scare me like that, Hayley. I thought something was seriously wrong."

"But, Mom, I--"

"That is enough, Hayley. Just stop." Amy sternly said, keeping her attention toward the table.

"I promise, Mom. I'm not making it up." Amy remained silent despite her daughter's plea.

Caroline grabbed napkins to begin cleaning the spilled drinks. She looked toward her sister and shook her head in disbelief. Hayley looked back at her sister, shocked and bothered that she obviously didn't believe her. Hayley stormed angrily out of the kitchen and back to her room. As she entered the room, the lingering smell of her drying vomit still filled the air. She quickly scrubbed what she could from the floor and sprayed an air freshener to rid the stench from the room.

As she set down the freshener can, her stomach erupted with pressure once again. She lifted her shirt and saw the same object moving inside of her again. Her heartbeat instantly burst to a sprint once again. She began to panic as she searched the room for anything that she thought could help. She fell onto her bed and slammed her hand against her stomach as hard as she could. The impact of her fist felt like nothing more than a small bump to her numbing stomach. The pounding was done to no avail as the hand continued to press and pry at her stomach. Unable to subdue the force, she lay on the bed and prayed that this horrifying event was not real.

A knock at the door stirred Hayley from her prayer. Caroline peeked around the door at her sister, a very concerned and fearful look on her face. "Hayley, are you alright?"

"No. No I'm not. I don't know what is wrong with me." Hayley said, gripping her stomach.

"I'm worried about you, Hay," Caroline's caring tone flowed from her easily as she walked across the room toward her sister, "First all the stuff that's happened at school, and now this. What's going on with you?"

"Caroline, I don't know. If I knew I wouldn't be so scared." Hayley groaned and rolled over onto her stomach.

Caroline stood watching her sister's discomfort. She rubbed her arm and jolted with pain when she touched her forearm. She examined what was causing the sting and found what appeared to be a large burn stretching the length of her right forearm. Her eyes widened at the sight of the injury. The burn, singed and sensitive, sat swollen and discolored from the rest of her light ivory skin. Caroline stared at her blistered arm in shock, "I- I have no idea how this happened! I never touched anything hot today."

Hayley turned over and inspected her sister's arm. Her eyes grew wide as she realized what the mark was. "Oh my god," she mumbled, "that's just like--" Her voice trailed off as she did not want to further alarm her sister. The shape of the scorched line was identical to the mark she left in her wall during her nightmare escape. Hayley sat in disbelief at what she witnessed on Caroline's arm.

"Just like what?" Caroline's voice shook, "Like what?!"

Hayley paused, not wanting to let her sister in on her revelation. Caroline would not believe her anyway after the kitchen incident. "Nothing," Hayley continued holding her stomach, "I thought it looked like something else."

"This is not the time for that, sis. I have to go talk to Mom." Caroline quickly darted from the room and down the stairs to the kitchen. Amy was scrubbing the dishes clean in the sink when her daughter came tearing around the corner. "Mom!"

Amy jumped, startled at the sudden shout behind her. "What is it, Caroline?"

"Mom, look at my arm!" Caroline thrust her arm forward revealing the long burn on her right forearm. Amy's brow creased in concern at the sight of the large scar.

"What happened? How did you get this?"

"I don't know. I can't remember anything happening. I just noticed it when I was upstairs." Caroline ran her fingers along the raised skin, wincing in pain as she hit sensitive areas of it.

"Caroline," she paused with an irritated look on her face, "just think. What did you do tonight that caused you to burn yourself?"

"Mom, I didn't do anything. This was not here earlier, I promise, it just showed up." Caroline's hands began shaking as she grew more frightened.

"Things like this don't just appear out of nowhere. What is going on with you girls? You've both been acting so strange lately."

Caroline tried to calm herself enough to explain, "Mom, I promise you, this was not here earlier tonight. As soon as Hayley went upstairs I went to check on her and that's when I saw it."

Amy grabbed her daughter's arm and examined the mark. "Well, it's definitely a solid burn. Let's put some aloe on it and see if we can't dull it a bit."

"I can't believe this, Mom. I'm supposed to go to New Orleans on Friday. I don't want to go with this ugly thing down my arm."

"Caroline, look, it's only a burn. You'll be fine. I know it's hot outside, but you could always wear sleeves if you really wanted to hide the mark." Amy grabbed the burn ointment from the cupboard and applied it to Caroline's arm. "Better?" Amy asked her daughter.

"Yeah, I guess it feels a little cooler now. I still don't know where it came from though. That's why I'm so scared about it."

"I don't know either, sweetheart. Keep trying to figure it out but, for now, I would like you to go check on your sister and make sure that she's doing alright. I'll be up when I finish down here."

"Alright, Mom."

Caroline left the kitchen, climbed the stairs, and approached her sister's room. She pressed her ear to the door and could hear no sound coming from inside. With two light knocks she slowly pushed the door open and peeked around the corner. Hayley lay motionless on the bed. Her body posed awkwardly across the bed. Caroline's heart sank at the sight of her sister. She darted across the floor to Hayley's bedside. "Hayley," she yelped while shaking her sister's shoulder, "are you alright?"

Hayley let out a deep groan and slightly lifted her head from the mattress. "What do you want?" she huffed.

"Sorry, Hay. I didn't see you move at all. I got scared 'cause of how you were acting before."

"I was sleeping," Hayley mumbled and set her head back down on the bed, "just let me be."

"Sorry, I will. Feel better." Caroline patted her sister on the shoulder before leaving her room. She closed the door silently behind herself and slipped back toward the kitchen, fighting concerned thoughts about her sister the whole way. The lights were off in the kitchen when she reached the bottom of the stairs. A dim glow of the television flickered from the nearby living room. Caroline saw her mother watching the news in the dark room and took a seat next to her on the couch.

"How's she doing?" Amy questioned.

"I'm not sure, she was asleep when I got up there. I didn't want to disturb her too much," Caroline dropped her head toward her lap, "I'm worried about her, Mom. She hasn't been herself at all lately."

"I know, Honey. I'm worried too. I wouldn't jump to any conclusions yet, though," Amy kept her attention on the television, "She may be having a rough time at school and it's just stressing her out."

"I realize that, but I feel like it's worse than she's letting on."

"How so?"

"I'm not entirely sure," Caroline paused, "This whole week she's been getting worse, and angrier, and more bitter."

"She's a senior. There's a lot of things coming down to the finish line soon for her."

Caroline nodded, her doubts ran rampant in her mind, "I don't know, Mom. I really think we need to keep a tight watch on her just in case."

"We will, Care. Just relax for now. Everything is going to be fine." Amy's words did little to comfort her daughter and quell her worries.

"Mom, I mean it, I-"

"Caroline." Amy sharply interrupted, "We will figure it out. Please, just relax for now. There's nothing we can do to instantly change it."

Caroline stood up from the couch, dissatisfied with her mother's vague concern for her own daughter and retreated to her room for the remainder of the evening.

= 15 =

Pens, pencils, markers, and paper. All strewn about Hayley's desk. She scribbled down verses of annoyance and desperation, hope and reality. During her feverish writing she knocked several of the pens and markers onto the floor. Fatigue began to set in as she wrote. She continued to write despite her dwindling energy. She lay her head down on her left arm and penned a few more lines. Her eyes grew heavier and she dozed off on her desk.

Hayley woke when her head suddenly dropped off her arm and bumped her desk. She blinked her eyes quickly to clear her vision. The drowsiness in her head refused to clear, she shook her head back and forth. Dropping her head toward her lap she rubbed her eyes and let out a long yawn. She gazed back to the papers on her desk. The words looked different now. Somehow blurred, yet still quite legible. She examined them and noticed something strange.   The edges of the words were slowly shifting shape, becoming more fluid and full of life.   Letters began lifting off of the page and floating into the air.   As the letters rose they dissipated into a deep gray smoke.   The dark vapor lingered over the desktop and surrounded Hayley's head.   She looked up into the small cloud above her head and watched as it shifted shapes and hung in the air.   Smoke continued to lift off the page into Hayley's face.   She inadvertently breathed in some of the lingering smoke and immediately began choking on it.   Her vision blurred and she began to feel very ill.

Hayley braced herself on the desk and slowly stood up from her seat.   Sweat developed on her forehead.   The room grew hotter and hotter by the minute.   She wiped the sweat off her brow and dabbed her wrist on her shirt.   Her attention was caught by a small pop sound behind her chair.   She spun around to see that her window curtains were on fire, burning from the floor upwards, and her eyes snapped wide open.   Sparks were breaking off and starting small fires across her bedroom.   She stood in shock at the sight of her bedroom burning to the ground.

The fire moved slowly across the floor like honey spilling from a jar, encompassing everything it touched. Hayley frantically began to search for something to smother the flames. She jumped to her bed and grabbed for her comforter. The second her hands touched the fabric it burst into flames. Hayley quickly snapped her hands back from the bed to avoid burning herself, stumbling backward as she did. Her foot slipped out from underneath her after stepping on a shoe near the bed, causing her to fall to the floor. She landed hard on her backside. She gathered herself and looked back toward the bed, her heart swiftly beating. Several burning footprints were left behind where she had stepped. Upon standing back to her feet, a nondescript burning shape flanked by two flaming handprints was left on the floor. The rising heat in her bedroom was bordering on unbearable.

Hayley felt her clothes begin to dampen with sweat. She rebuilt her composure and moved back toward the bed. The fire upon her bed spread across the width of the mattress and down to the bed. The flames engulfed the entire bed and frame in a matter of seconds. She watched in horror as her whole bedroom was soon completely enveloped in flames. Careful not to touch anything she backed out of the room, each step leaving a scorching footprint behind. With every passing second more and more fires sparked.

She walked backwards through her doorway. As she passed through the opening the trim surrounding the door sparked and popped. The wood trim began to smoke and seconds later flames seeped from the planks and inundated the whole doorway. She turned and looked down the hallway. The hellish glow emanating from the burning room and doorway lit the dark corridor. Small details of the doors to the other rooms were barely visible, hidden in the escaping smoke and remaining darkness. The hallway stairs, just feet away, were nearly completely hidden in the darkness. Hayley moved along close to the wall and deeper into the shadows. She slid her hand along the wall, her fingers leaving fiery streaks that carved into the drywall.

Gazing behind herself, back toward the flames, she saw the flames following. Every step she took, the fires inched along the wall. Its thick black smoke lifting up to the ceiling, creating a night-like sky inside her home. She again peered into the darkness ahead. The shadows appeared to shift like something within them was moving. Coming from her room the sound of cracking and crumbling wood could be heard. Hayley squinted her eyes, trying to see what was caused the stir. She could not see anything ahead of her.

"Caroline?" Hayley called out, "Mom?" No answer from either of them. A deep breath filled her lungs as she marched on into the darkness. The dim glow of the flames behind her continued to light her immediate area while leaving the space ahead devoid of light. She shuffled her feet, making sure to keep contact with the floor at all times. She felt her toe slip off the edge of the top stair. Slowly she lowered her foot onto the next step and placed her hand on the railing to the right. Her hand gripped the rail tightly. The edge of her hand began to glow as the wood beneath her palm started to burn. A small flame flickered up from in between her middle and index fingers. The small ember split into two and soon three and four. Her entire palm quickly filled with flames it could not contain any longer. The flame spilled down the hand rail igniting the length of the bar. Light filled the hall, lifting the dark veil covering the hallway.

Hayley continued down the stairs and into the kitchen, her steps continually illuminating her way. She tried to flip the light switch for the room but the switch did not work as her hand ignited and melted the plastic plate. The kitchen remained dim, lit only by the glow off her past footsteps and handprints. She turned away from the kitchen and toward the front door. The fires behind her had filled the whole stairwell. Deep gray smoke completely masked the ceiling overhead.

"Go." A voice called out. Hayley sharply jumped at the sudden interruption. "Go." The voice called again. She now recognized the voice as her own, calling out to her from the smoke. Her heart began to race.

"Hello?" Hayley piped.

"Get out." The voice whispered.

Hayley began to search for a way out of the smoke and fire filled room. Her eyes locked straight ahead to the front door. With five quick bounding steps she ran to the door. She grabbed and wrenched on the doorknob. Locked. Quickly she turned the lock and deadbolt before turning the knob again. The door remained sturdily shut. Hayley turned around and saw the fire growing ever more intense and closing in on her, surrounding her. She repeatedly yanked the door but to no avail. Jumping back she pounded her hand on the door. "Help!" She cried out, "Somebody!"

She continued to smash her fist into the wooden body of the door. Pound after pound, punch after punch, Hayley gave all she had into hitting the door. The deep pounding of her fist echoed across the entry way. "Anybody!" she howled. Hayley took a few steps back from the door, took a deep breath and lowered her shoulder. With all of her energy she slammed her shoulder into the door. Her body crashed into the solid wood. Again and again she tried to break through the door. "Get out," the voice whispered once more.

Hayley increased her efforts and exertion. After seven attempts the wood of the door began to give. Hayley put her hands on her knees and tried to catch her breath. Sweat dripped from her face and onto the floor, sizzling on impact. She lifted her head back toward the door and stood erect. Hayley glanced to her feet, her black running shoes looked like silhouettes against the flame lit floor. She patted her fist on her hip in determination. Placing one foot behind her and opening her hips she lurched forward and slammed her heel into the crack near the door's latch. Once, twice, three times more. The wood began to splinter under the impact of her foot. Her fourth kick broke a small hole through the door. Regaining her breath, she leaned back again. *One more should do the trick.* With every bit of her energy she gave it one more forceful kick. A small portion of the door, big enough for Hayley to squeeze through, splintered away from the frame revealing the front porch and an much needed escape route.

Smoke poured out of the fresh hole in the door. Hayley turned her body and squeezed through the small opening, catching and tearing the right shoulder of her shirt on the sharp splinters. She pushed against the door frame until she was able to pull her legs through. Fresh air filled her lungs with deep, refreshing breaths. Hayley propped herself up onto one knee, brushing the dirt and ashes from her pants. The front yard of the house was pitch dark, lit only by the dim glow of the fires inside the house. She pulled herself to her feet and hunched over with her hands on her knees. Her breathing heavy at first, slowly returning to her normal pace. Hayley's heart was finally able to slow and she could fully regain her composure.

The flames her footsteps had been leaving behind no longer appeared and her sweat began to dissipate. Hayley focused her vision ahead and started to walk away from her burning home. She glanced back only once. The burning door crumbled away from its hinges and fell to the ground in a pile of ashes. Black smoke continued to pour out of the house as the flames inside devoured everything in sight. Hayley turned away again and proceeded to walk away from the porch. Her stride began to slow and become more and more difficult. She struggled to lift her feet from the pavement as if they were chained to the ground. Soon her feet were rendered completely immobile.

Hayley tried as hard as she could to lift her feet off of the ground but she was unable to move them. Nothing she could see appeared to be holding them to the ground. Hayley grabbed her ankle, trying to tear it from the ground, with all of her force she could not budge it an inch. A hot breeze blew over Hayley's back and caused her to stand straight up. Her shoulders twitched backward as the hot wind shifted back toward the house. Her hair flowed in the sharp breeze. The wind grew stronger, tugging at her clothes. Hayley leaned forward to brace herself against the increasingly intense winds. The forceful gusts knocked Hayley back, pulling her feet off the ground. She felt something grip her shoulders and snapped her head to see what it was. Nothing could be seen when she looked but she could feel the cold fingers pressing into her skin. Her shirt showed the imprint of hands gripping her body. The grasp tightened to a painful level before she reached to attempt to pry the invisible hands from her shoulders.

Hayley swung her hand up to her shoulder, however, she could feel nothing there. Her fingers slipped into the impressions caused by the ghostly grip. It remained latched on to her but she could not feel it with her own hands. The grip upon her shoulders grew tighter and Hayley let out a strained yelp as she lowered her body toward the ground trying to escape the grasp. Tears formed in the corners of her eyes and rolled down her cheeks. She fell to the ground, landing on her backside. The clutch upon her shoulders did not yield for a second. Hayley felt her body being pulled and tried to grab at anything to stop herself. She was out of reach of anything that could help. The force dragged her along the porch back toward the front of the house, her heels grinding along.

Her feet repeatedly slipped on the concrete porch like a car with bald tires. The heat from the burning house singed Hayley's neck as she was dragged back in through the doorway. She kicked her legs wildly as she struggled to escape. Grabbing at the small scorched posts left where the door once stood, her fingernails bent backwards from the pressure of her clutch. Ashes from the crumbled door stained the bottom of her shirt and pants with a dark gray dust.

Smoke continued to fill the rooms and cover the ceiling. The force holding her hostage aggressively threw Hayley down to the lower level, clearing all of the steps on the way down. Her body flew through the air like a rag doll and slammed into the floor, scattering ashes in every direction. A large gasp of air was forced from Hayley's lungs upon impact. She rolled over onto her knees trying to regain her breath. Slowly and painfully her lungs filled again and she was able to boost herself up to her knees. Hayley looked around her burned out home. Walls had crumbled and the stairs had begun to collapse on themselves.

Air in the living room began to swirl around Hayley. The wind tossed her hair and whipped at her now dirty and tattered clothes. Three small piles of ashes developed around Hayley. She looked at them confused as they started to move and change shape. Flames spun around the ash piles causing them to grow up from the floor. The dark piles formed into the shape of people. The spiraling flames intensified and spun faster. Hayley took a step backward from the flaming towers. The flames subsided and disappeared, leaving the glowing humanlike ash mounds behind. Bit by bit the ashes blew away revealing Hayley's family. First Eli's face appeared from the dust, then Amy, and finally Caroline.

"Hayley!" Cried Caroline.

Hayley's eyes sprung open, "Caroline!" she yelped, "Mom, Dad!"

"Help us, Hayley," Eli pleaded, "You've got to help us."

Hayley's eyes welled with tears, "How can I do that?"

"You've got to fight." Amy demanded through tears.

"Fight what?" Hayley questioned. Her hands began to shake.

"Fight it." The three of them responded in unison.

"Fight what?!" She cried.

"Fight. Fight. Fight" They continued, their voices dull and lifeless. Their eyes glassed over and faces expressionless.

"What do I have to fight?" Hayley fell to her knees and sobbed. She grasped a pile of ashes in her hand.

"Do not let it win. You cannot give in." Caroline begged.

"I- I," Hayley tried to find the words to say, "I won't. I'll never give up."

"Hayley," Amy called out, "help--" Amy's skin began to glow. The light beneath her skin grew brighter and brighter. Her skin split open releasing flames from her shoulders that quickly consumed her whole body.

"No!" Cried Hayley.

"Help." Eli whispered as he was also overtaken by the flames. Caroline soon met the same fate. The family members burned for a short moment before falling back into piles of ashes. Hayley dropped her head to the floor and sobbed uncontrollably.

She lifted her head and shook the sleep from her eyes. Her heart raced as she looked around her bedroom. Sweat lined her forehead. The lamp on her desk gave the room a warm golden glow. Outside her window the clear night sky showed few stars surrounding the bright moon. Nothing in her room was out of the ordinary. She stood up from her seat and explored her room. She looked all around the room, but not a single piece of furniture was out of place. Hayley peeked out into the hallway to check for fires. Her brow furrowed in confusion at the now realized nightmare she had just suffered through. *What in the world is going?* Exhausted and weary Hayley collapsed into her bed.

= *16* =

Caroline awoke in the middle of the night. She rubbed the sleep from her eyes and looked around her bedroom. Everything hidden in the cloak of midnight darkness. A steady bumping sounded through her wall. Caroline perked her head up against her headboard and tried to figure out the origin of the sound. She patted her hand along her nightstand looking for the switch of the lamp. Her fingers clipped the switch and she flicked the light on. Her eyes immediately squinted at the sudden burst of light. Once her eyes adjusted to the light she scanned her room yet saw nothing out of the ordinary. The sound was emanating from the shared wall between Hayley's room and her own. Caroline slipped off of her bed and walked over to the wall. She placed her ear against the light blue facade. The knocking continued in a steady rhythm. She lightly tapped her fist against the wall three times to see if it would interrupt the sound or catch the attention of her sister. The noise did not subside for one second, continuing in its eerie monotonous tempo. No other sounds could be heard through the wall.

Caroline, confused and alarmed, lifted her head from the wall and walked to her door. She quietly opened the door and peeked down the hallway. A flickering glow like that of a candle seeped out from under Hayley's door. The curious tapping persisted. Taking a deep breath, Caroline slid from her room and snuck to her sister's door. She pressed her ear against the door, more constant bumping sounds. A faint voice caught her attention. Not a word could be picked out of the hushed mumbling. Caroline knocked lightly on the door, hoping her sister would acknowledge her presence. No answer. Her nerves grew as she waited for a response. She knocked again, nothing. Caroline reached for the door knob and quietly opened the door.

Poking her head inside Caroline saw her sister's bed pushed away from the wall. She cautiously walked into the candlelit room. Her sister sat with her back against the wall behind the bed. Hayley sat with her arms wrapped around her knees pulled into her chest. She mumbled incoherent sentences of apparent gibberish while hitting her head into the wall. Papers laid strewn about the room. The mysterious notebook laid open on the floor in front of Hayley, pages ripped from its spine. A small mound of ashes rested on some of the loose pages of the notebook. Caroline's eyes widened at the sight of her sister. She darted to Hayley and knelt down near her.

"Hayley," she said quietly, "Hayley?" Hayley did not respond. She kept mumbling and bumping her head against the wall as Caroline continued to reach for her attention. "Hayley, are you alright?"

Silence. Heart wrenching, deafening, mind crushing silence.

Hayley stopped moving, stopped hitting her head, stopped murmuring. Caroline's eyes began to burn and well with tears. "Hayley!" she gasped. Hayley sat stiff and motionless against the bedroom wall. Caroline's hands shook violently as her heart dropped. A single tear rolled down her cheek and into the corner of her mouth. The salty droplet rested on her quivering lip before falling to the floor. Hayley's seemingly lifeless body lay still in front of her sister.

Caroline reached out her shaking hand to grab her sister and felt a sharp slap across her arm as Hayley snapped awake. The swipe left three large scratches across Caroline's forearm. She winced in pain as she snapped her arm back. Hayley's eyes, opened wider than Caroline had ever seen, sharply turned and locked on her terrified sister. All color had drained from Hayley's eyes as they filled with opaque black smoke. Caroline sat frozen, tears halted in her eyes, unable to divert her gaze from her sister. Hayley's devilish ebony eyes looked straight into Caroline's soul. A deep rumbling growl began to grow in Hayley's throat as she held her lifeless stare. The evil sound grew louder with each passing second. Hayley's lips pulled back exposing her teeth as her mouth curled into a beastly sneer. Caroline's breathing escalated to a near uncontrollable level watching her sister appear to transform into some sort of inhuman creature. She braced both of her arms on the floor behind her back as Hayley slowly lifted her head from the wall.

"Hayley? What's wrong with you? You're scaring me."

Her sister said nothing. Only horrific growls left her mouth.

"Mom! Help!" Caroline cried out.

Hayley's shoulders pulled off of the wall. Caroline leaned her weight back on her arms as her sister moved closer. Hayley lifted her arm and placed her hand firmly on the mattress. She let out a deep growl followed by a loud clack of her jaw before pressing her hand deep into the cushion of the bed. Caroline slipped her feet back and placed them flat on the floor. Not knowing what to expect she called for her mother again, "Mom! Get in here now!"

"Caroline?!" Amy called back.

"Mom! Help me!"

Caroline brought her full attention back to her sister. Hayley's hand gripped the mattress so tight the sheets and cloth began to tear beneath her fingernails. She lurched forward, fire exploding in her eyes, throwing her body straight at Caroline. Her hands nearly reached her sister's throat before she was stopped mid leap by Caroline's foot. Caroline pressed against Hayley's chest with her foot with all of her might. She grunted and groaned, straining to keep herself at a safe distance while her sister clawed and grasped for her face and neck. Hayley strained to get at her victim but remained restrained no matter her effort.

Amy came bounding into the room, catching her daughters mid-battle. "Girls! Enough!" she yelled.

Hayley continued to reach for her sister's throat. Her hands inched closer and closer as Caroline tired from the pressure. Hayley's nails grazed Caroline's soft neck before she was able to muster enough remaining energy to forcibly shove Hayley back against the wall with her leg. Hayley's head slammed into the wall, leaving a large dent and crack in the drywall. Her body went limp immediately after the impact. Her eyes rested half open as saliva fell from her lips.

Caroline jumped to her feet and ran to her mother, tears pouring down her face. Her mother's frantic emotions were glaringly apparent. "What's wrong, Caroline?" She shook as she searched for answers to her daughter's cries.

"It's Hayley!" Caroline, trying to subdue her tears, pointed to her sister's motionless body, "She was sitting there then jumped at me out of nowhere and I pushed her back and she just stopped moving."

Amy held her daughter against her chest. Looking across the room she saw Hayley's unconscious body. Her own eyes filled with horrified tears. With three large running steps she got down to her daughter's side and attempted to revive her. "Hayley! Come back to me, sweetie," She patted Hayley's shoulders and legs, "please come back."

Caroline watched her mother's attempts, praying for something to work. Glancing down to the floor, she spied one of the torn up pages at her feet. Her tears made it nearly impossible to see anything clearly. She picked up the page piece, wiped away her tears, and examined it. Some of the mysterious message remained. The edges of the paper were singed a deep brown where they broke off from the main body of the page. Her vision slowly cleared as her tears faded. Only fragments of most words were visible except for one: *Prison.* Her mind began to twist and turn as to what the remainder of the page could have said. Maybe it was something awful, maybe not. Maybe it was nothing. She folded the scorched piece and placed it in her pajamas' pocket.

Snapping back to reality she continued to watch her mother try to wake Hayley. "Mom, we have to get her to the hospital," she pulled at her mother's shoulder, "they're the only ones who can help right now."

"You're right. Let's go right now," Amy climbed to her feet, "Help me carry her to the car."

Caroline helped lift Hayley with her mother. Amy carried Hayley's upper body while Caroline held her feet off of the ground. Slowly and determined, they carried Hayley all the way downstairs. Caroline reached one hand away to unlock and open the front door. She grabbed the car keys off of the coat hook near the door before grabbing Hayley's legs again. Minimal street lights and house lights were visible in the dark of the night. They carried Hayley's body around the front of the house to Amy's car. Amy slipped into the car and pulled Hayley head first into the back seat with her. Amy placed the jacket from the floor of the crimson sedan under Hayley's head as a makeshift pillow. "Sit in the front but keep your eyes on Hayley to watch for any changes," she instructed Caroline, "The bumpiness of the ride might shake her awake."

"Got it. Let's go, Mom."

Amy jumped into the driver's seat, slammed the door shut, and started the engine. "Hold on," she said to Caroline, "might be a little rough." She firmly pressed the gas pedal down and the car sped off. The force of the car turning out of the driveway pushed Caroline up against her door. Amy accelerated down the street, recklessly ignoring the stop signs in the neighborhood. She sped along, her emotions racing as fast as her car. Turning out of her neighborhood she continued her frantic pace toward the hospital.

The midnight traffic was very sparse, leaving many roads wide open. The short drive to the hospital felt like an eternity to Amy and Caroline. A small number of cars lined the parking lot of the hospital. The large white building shined like a light from the gods against the starless night sky. Amy pulled the car right up to the doors of the emergency room and parked. "Wait here," she commanded Caroline, "I'll get help." She sprinted from the car and into the building.

Caroline looked back to her sister, "It's going to be alright, Hayley," she said holding her sister's hand, "Mom went to get help. It's going to okay. It's has to be." Her voice began to shake as Amy came darting back out of the emergency room with two nurses behind her.

The nurses brought a gurney with them to the side of the car. "I'm going to need both of you to step aside," one nurse directed

Amy and Caroline. The nurses carefully loaded Hayley onto the bed and wheeled her inside. They immediately took her into a room at the end of the hall and began to examine her. A nurse stayed behind to begin questioning Amy about her daughter.

"My name is Meredith. I am going to need you to answer a few questions for me."

"Okay," Amy replied, "I'm Amy."

"Alright, Amy," Meredith began, "please tell me exactly what happened to your daughter."

"We aren't actually sure. My other daughter was the one who yelled for me when it happened."

Meredith turned to Caroline, "Can you tell me what happened?"

"I'll try. I was in my room and heard a noise coming from my sister's room." Caroline then began explaining the strange events from earlier in the night. "I walked into the hallway and saw a light on in her room so I poked my head in and saw her sitting next to her bed."

"Okay, then what?" Meredith said while writing things on her clipboard.

"Then I walked over to her and she was hitting her head into the wall. I tried to get her to stop but she wouldn't listen to me. Then she just went limp."

"She just stopped moving? No signs of injury or anything like that?"

"Not that I could really tell," Caroline continued to explain, "I was too scared to really check. I went to grab her to try and wake her up but she snapped awake and slapped my hand away."

"That is very strange. What else?"

"After she hit me I noticed that her eyes were all black and she was growling. Like a weird deep growl, not like a dog. That's when she jumped at me and tried to attack me."

"What do you mean she attacked you?" Meredith questioned.

"She jumped and tried to grab me, so I fell back and pushed her with my foot. I knocked her back against the wall and she hit her head. That's when she stopped moving again and she hasn't moved at all since then."

"Okay, we'll definitely have to run some tests for a head injury then."

"Do you know what could have made her act like that?"

"We won't really know anything until we run some tests, but it could be anything from a head injury to drugs to even something similar to sleep walking. We won't know for sure until later."

Meredith asked Amy a few more general questions about Hayley before walking down the hall into another room.

"Mom, we have to do something." Caroline implored, grabbing her mother's arm.

"There's nothing we can do right now, Caroline. She's where she needs to be."

Caroline released her grip and took a seat along the wall. Amy, trying to be strong for her daughter, stood quietly in the center of the waiting room. She folded her arms across her chest to hide her nervous, fidgeting hands. A lump sat in her throat at the thought of possibly losing her daughter. The next few agonizing minutes seemed like hours until Meredith returned.

"We've got Hayley all settled in her room. You can go and see her now. We will be in shortly to run a few initial tests." She smiled and left the waiting room.

"Thank you, Meredith." Amy replied and signaled to Caroline to come along. The two of them walked down the brightly lit hallway to Hayley's room. Hayley lay motionless on the hospital bed, wires attached to her body. Monitors sat at both sides of the small white bed. Caroline and Amy entered the room and walked to Hayley's side. Amy's eyes welled with tears at the sight of her daughter. She covered her mouth with her hand as she placed the other on her daughter's side. "I love you," Amy whispered, "please come back to us."

Caroline sat in the chair next to the bed with her head bowed. She prayed silently for her sister's recovery before standing at her mother's side. Amy's hand pressed against Caroline's back. Her touch provided a small sense of comfort for Caroline. A sense of family, a sense of normalcy, a sense of hope. Hope that everything would be alright.

Caroline turned to her mother, "She's going to be okay, right?"

"She's going to be fine, sweetheart. We have to let the doctors do everything they can."

"I know. I'm scared, though. I can't see her like this."

"She will be alright, Caroline. We won't give up until she is. Just try to settle down for now."

Caroline nodded and went back to the chair beside the bed. She rested her elbows on the arm rests and placed her hands on her head. A single tear rolled down her cheek and fell to the white tile floor. Her lips began to quiver but her attention was pulled away by the sound of the door opening. Meredith came back in the room with her trusty clipboard. She checked the monitors around Hayley's bed, making marks on her papers after carefully checking each. Caroline watched Meredith as she worked. Her light blue scrubs nearly blended in with the bedding covering Hayley. Meredith made a few final marks before turning to Amy. "I'll be right back, I just need to pass along these numbers." She said and left the room.

"Do you think that everything is okay?" Caroline asked.

"I can't be certain but she didn't look or sound too concerned with what she was writing," Amy replied, "so I think things are as good as they can be at this point."

"I hope so."

Meredith strolled back into Hayley's room. "Okay, here's where we stand with Hayley right now." she explained, "We aren't completely sure what the cause is yet, but her levels seem to be right around normal. Whatever happened doesn't look like it has had much effect on her. As she has not regained consciousness we obviously need to keep her here until she does."

Amy nodded, "I understand. We will do whatever is necessary to get her back."

"I figured as much," Meredith smiled, "you can stay as long as you need to. We will keep checking on her to see if there are any changes in her condition."

"Thank you, Meredith."

Caroline stood up as Meredith left the room again and walked over to the window and looked out at the dimly lit streets. The streets were eerily empty at this hour of the night. Hope of a new day and renewed hope for her sister filled her heart.

= *17* =

Light slowly warmed the sky as the sun rose. Caroline jumped as she felt a hand grab her shoulder. She turned to see her mother's face next to her, eyes red, with a half smile peeking through the pain. "It's time to go, sweetheart," Amy said softly, "you've got to get to school today."

"What?" Caroline turned to face her mother, eyes wide open, "No, Mom. We have to stay here with Hayley."

"Caroline, us being here won't do anything until she's awake again. She's where she needs to be."

"But, Mom-"

"The people here are the ones who can help her. We will come back every day to visit her, I promise."

"Alright," Caroline reluctantly agreed, "let's go then."

"Plus," Amy added, "you know they won't let you go on the New Orleans trip tomorrow if you aren't in school."

"Yeah, I know," Caroline drooped her shoulders and walked to her sister's bedside, "Hayley, we have to get going now. We'll be back every day, I promise," resting her hand on Hayley's forehead she whispered, "I love you."

The early summer heat came fast in the morning hours that day. The sun cooked the dark pavement below. Stagnant air and stifling humidity made for a sickening morning drive. Caroline stared out of the window as Amy drove them both home, watching each passing car and building with an empty mind. Her emotions had pulled any remaining energy from her body. Mental exhaustion had already set in and would make for an awfully long day.

After a quick stop at home to clean up and grab their things, Amy and Caroline climbed back into the car and drove away. Early morning talk radio provided the soundtrack to the otherwise exhausted silence of the ride. Moments later Amy turned into the Theroux High School parking lot and pulled up toward the front of the building to drop off her daughter. Caroline grabbed the door handle to exit but felt her mother's hand grab her arm. "Just take it easy today, okay?" Amy said softly.

"I will, Mom. Let me know if you hear anything."

"Of course, sweetheart. Just make it through today and we'll go see her. Then you can have some fun on your trip tomorrow."

Caroline let a doubtful laugh slip out, "I'll try. Bye, Mom."

"Bye, Care."

Amy watched her daughter walk away until she disappeared into the building. With a sigh, Amy pulled out of the parking lot and headed to work. Thoughts of her infirmed daughter flooded her mind. Her mind could not waver from the painful images of her own child unconscious on the hospital bed. Guilt soon followed the pain. She wondered if there was anything she could have done to stop what happened. She still had no idea what happened and wondered if the doctors would actually be able to find anything. Hayley seemed so healthy that same night. In the blink of an eye, her life was turned upside down by something unknown, something unseen. Amy viciously cranked the volume on the radio in a feeble attempt to drown out the horrible pain and guilt in her mind and heart.

Her eyes began to tremble with tears as she drove through town. She wiped them on her shirt attempted to hold herself together despite her fragile mental state. Nothing could put her mind at rest this morning. The only hope she could muster from this tragedy was the outside chance that work could take her mind off her heartache, if only for an instant. Insisting on going to work felt like a betrayal against her daughter, however, there was nothing else she could do. Hayley remained unresponsive in the only place that could help her get healthy again. Amy's presence would not help speed the process at all.

The city seemed less alive that day. Amy knew in her heart that nothing would be the same until her daughter was back to normal. Everything was quickly put into perspective. Her job, her money, her home, nothing held the same kind of value it once had. Amy's office came into view as she continued down the road. Amy let out a heavy-hearted sigh as she parked her car. She closed her eyes and gave a silent prayer. Her breathing got deeper and her face began to burn as tears welled in her eyes. Her emotions hit her like wrecking ball. Completely overwhelmed, she lost control of her heart and cried heavy and hard.

Amy was startled by a knock on her window. She jumped and looked out, wiping her eyes she saw Laurie, her coworker and longtime friend. The concern in Laurie's eyes was obvious. She was oblivious to the horrible events of the night before. Amy opened her door and stood to meet Laurie.

"Amy, what's wrong?"

Amy wrapped her arms around Laurie and sobbed for a moment before regaining some of her composure. "It's Hayley," Amy said, "She's in the hospital."

"That's terrible! What happened?" Laurie questioned.

"We don't really know. Caroline said something about Hayley acting really strange and then trying to attack her. It's all very bizarre."

"That is very odd," Laurie replied shaking her head, "I don't know if I've ever heard of anything like that before."

"Me either. That's basically what the hospital has told us too. It has made this whole ordeal much scarier since we don't know what's going on with her."

"Have they given any guess as to what it could possibly be?"

"No. They haven't found anything yet. She's only been there since early this morning. I haven't slept since she got there."

Grabbing Amy's shoulder Laurie tried to offer any bit of comfort that she could muster. "Well she's in the right place for now."

"I know, it's just so hard." Amy's voice shook as her tears returned. She pressed her head into Laurie's shoulder and let her grief out. "I hope that Caroline is able get through her day better than I can." Laurie comforted Amy until she was able to regain a bit of her composure and quell her tears.

Caroline's morning wasn't any easier than her mother's. Lectures and lesson plans were nothing more than static noise behind Caroline's wandering mind. Nothing she tried would take her focus off of Hayley. The image of her lying in that hospital bed was carved into her brain, a constant reminder of the pain she was feeling. Every minute was grindingly slow and seemed to last forever.

First period came to a close and Caroline sulked to the hallway, eyes fixed on the floor. Her stride was broken when she walked head first into someone's back. She snapped to attention and saw that she nearly knocked the person off of their feet. "Oh jeez, I'm sorry!" Caroline exclaimed.

Her unintentional victim turned around chuckling. "That's alright, Caroline." Devin. Of course. Of all people that she could have bumped into at school, it had to be the person her sister talked about most. As if it wasn't hard enough to not think of her sister's condition without seeing her friends, now she was face to face with one.

"Oh, Devin, hey," Caroline sheepishly piped, "how's it going?"

"It's going alright, how are you? Where's your sister today? I haven't seen her anywhere."

Caroline dipped her eyes away from Devin's, "Not great. She's in the hospital."

"Wait. What?" Devin interrupted, "What happened?"

"I wish I knew," Caroline began walking down the hall with Devin in tow, "she was acting extra strange, then just stopped."

Devin grabbed Caroline's arm, stopping her in the middle of the hall, "What do you mean 'just stopped?"

"I don't know what really happened. She was acting almost like an animal, then tried to attack me. I pushed her off and she just went limp. She hasn't moved since then."

"So she's still out cold? Have the doctors said anything?"

"They've tried a lot of different tests on her so far, but haven't found any answers yet."

Devin eyes searched the empty air for answers, "I'm so confused, how don't they have any answers yet?"

"Your guess is as good as mine, really," Caroline adjusted her backpack on her shoulders, "I've got to go though, I'm going to see her after school, so hopefully I'll have some better news then."

"Let me know any news if you can."

"I will. Bye, Devin." Caroline disappeared into the crowded hallway. Devin stepped back against the lockers lining the hallway, resting his head on the cool metal. His stomach quaked with a rush of nerves, a level concern that surprised himself. He stood against the lockers until the bell caught his attention. Clutching his bag he jogged down the hall to his next class.

Caroline quietly rode through her day hoping to avoid any unnecessary conversations and reasons to bring up her sister's current state. Class slowly began to feel like relief rather than a task. It provided a chance for her to try and focus her mind on something else, a stark contrast to how her day started. Assignments shifted her focus and allowed her to relax, as minimal as it may have been. While talking with her friends she made sure to avoid any topics that would lead to conversations of family or family happenings.

During lunch it proved increasingly difficult for Caroline to hide her emotions like a slowly growing fire. Her close friends had grown to know Hayley very well over the years and would often ask about her. Caroline sluggishly picked at her food. Her friends quickly realized that their normally perky friend was oddly quiet today. She reluctantly explained what was going on with her sister to them. After going through the minimal details she had, her friends remained quiet and confused.

"I know, I'm as confused as you guys," Caroline sheepishly chuckled, "I'm supposed to be going to see her after school today. Hopefully I'll actually find out what's going on."

"Keep your head up, Care," her friend Dez remarked, "Everything is going to be alright."

"I'm trying to. Not the easiest thing I've done, by far." The bell sounded and the students cleared the cafeteria. Caroline let out a slow blow breath and stood up from her table, "Two hours," she whispered to herself, "two hours."

= *18* =

Amy arrived at Theroux shortly after the final bell sounded. She took the remainder of her day off to pick up Caroline and get to the hospital as early as possible. Her quiet desperation had dwindled throughout the day to be replaced by a cautious optimism. She let out a long but quiet yawn while waiting for her daughter. A horrid night followed by a long day of heavy emotion had worn her energy level to almost zero.

Caroline slowly sauntered from the school, Devin at her side. Amy watched as they chatted while walking, said their goodbyes and separated. Caroline turned and opened the back door of the car and dropped her bag inside. With a half smile on her face she took her seat next to her mother.

"How are you doing?" Amy asked.

"I'm doing alright right now," Caroline answered, "it wasn't easy today, but I'm okay."

"Good. Hopefully we can get some answers from them today." Amy pulled away from the curb, "Let's go see her."

"I hope so," Caroline dropped her head, "I'm ready for something positive."

"Were you talking to Devin about it?"

"Yeah," Caroline looked to her mother, "I figured he should know what was going on since those two have become pretty close recently."

Amy nodded, "Was he worried?"

Caroline let out a small laugh, "I guess so. He seemed concerned when I told him, I think. He didn't really say much after that."

"So what did you two talk about when you were coming to the car?" Amy questioned.

"I just told him that we were going to see her now and he just told me to let him know what we find out." Caroline continued, "So he gave me his number and told me to call or text him after we leave the hospital."

"Well that's nice of him to worry about her." Amy smiled, "I didn't know they had gotten close to each other."

"I don't know," Caroline sighed, "ever since they went out after the art show they've talked almost every day." She laughed as she continued, "I'm not sure where they stand, but Hayley hasn't shut up about it since."

Amy chuckled, "Sounds to me like she's into him."

Caroline laughed more, "Obviously."

Amy pulled the car into the hospital parking lot. She turned off the engine and looked to her daughter, "You ready?"

"Yeah, I'm ready." Caroline opened her door and exited into the hot sun.

The bright white lights and matching floor of the hospital waiting area was always unnerving to Caroline. It was a cold unwelcoming room. A quiet space where nervous tension filled the air. Every person in the waiting area had the same solemn look of concern carved into their face. Mothers, fathers, and siblings of unseen patients waited for news of their condition. Caroline examined them all, trying to feel for them. She was unable to do so. Her mind was already overflowing with her own fret and thoughts of what the doctors could tell her. Good or bad, she was ready to know what was going on.

Amy and Caroline marched through the waiting room toward Hayley's room. The door to her room opened as they approached and Meredith exited along with a doctor. They were talking but too quietly for Amy to hear from her distance. Meredith turned and saw Caroline and Amy heading her way and gave them both a shy crooked smile, "Hi, ladies."

"Hi, Meredith," Amy greeted, "and doctor."

"How are you today, Amy? This is Dr. Jefferies" Meredith raised her hand signaling to the man on her right. A tall, dark skinned man in a fresh white lab coat.

"Hello doctor. I've been better, Meredith. How are things with Hayley going?" Amy questioned.

Meredith lifted her clipboard to her face to read the test results, "This isn't easy, but we haven't seen any change at all in Hayley's condition."

Amy shook her head in disbelief, "What do you mean no change?"

"Well, everything is the same as when she came in here," Meredith continued, "although we have noticed a couple things that stuck out as strange."

"What do you mean?" Amy's brow creased, "Strange how?"

Dr. Jefferies cleared his throat, "Well, we've run extensive tests throughout the day to figure out what is going on with your daughter and so far have found nothing." Amy tried to get a word in but Dr. Jefferies continued before she could, "Two things stood out as a constant of every test."

"What are they?" Caroline piped.

"While Hayley is unresponsive to nearly everything, all of her vitals remain stable and show no signs of distress."

"What does that mean?" Amy chimed in.

"It's a peculiar event. Most times we will find something in our tests that will at least point us in the right direction. So far," Dr. Jefferies turned the page of his clipboard, "so far, our heart rate, breathing, and blood pressure tests have matched that of a healthy person."

"So does that mean that nothing is wrong?" Asked Caroline.

"Not necessarily, as Meredith mentioned, there is another strange piece to this puzzle." Dr. Jefferies turned another page, "According to our scans, while her other tests were normal, her brain activity is off the charts."

"I'm confused," said Amy, "so she's not able to do anything but her mind is going crazy?"

"That is how it appears right now. We are still searching for the answer," the doctor elaborated, "her mind is fighting as hard as it can, but something is fighting back just as hard and keeping her this way. It is as if she is very intensely dreaming during periods of the day. She doesn't move her extremities or make any noise when it happens, but her eyes move very rapidly. This is similar to R.E.M. sleep and yet different because her heart rate and breathing remain unchanged."

Amy's head spun from the information she just received, "Do you have any idea how long she could be like this?"

"Unfortunately, it's impossible to know. I'm sorry but there is no way to tell." Dr. Jefferies closed his clipboard and put it to his side, "I have to go now. We will keep working until we find the answer for this. You have my word."

"Thank you, doctor," Amy graciously said.

"I'm very sorry we didn't have more of an answer for you." Meredith said with a solemn tone.

"It's alright, Meredith," Amy assured, "It's all very confusing to me, but it's also only been one day."

"I promise you we're doing everything we can to get to the bottom of this. It is a very peculiar thing for us to encounter as well," Meredith fiddled with her charts, "I'll be popping in and out for the next few minutes comparing results. Feel free to stay as long as you would like."

"Thank you, Meredith." Amy directed Caroline into Hayley's room and took a seat next to her daughter's bed. She placed her hand on Hayley's hand, stroking her fingers with her thumb. "We're here again, sweety," Amy whispered, "please come back to us."

Caroline sat alongside her mother, her eyes wandered the brightly lit room. "Mom," Caroline whispered, "I don't think I should go tomorrow."

"You're going, Care. You need to. There's nothing much either of us can do here." Amy smiled at her daughter's thoughtfulness. "I know why you want to stay, and I appreciate you wanting to be here for your sister."

"No, Mom, I-" Caroline tried to interrupt.

"Caroline," Amy laughed, "You're going. You need to go have some fun with your friends."

Caroline sighed and accepted her mother's ruling. "I'll try."

Amy and Caroline stayed with Hayley through the local news. They shared the stories of their days with her, hoping the familiar voices would help draw her back. Hayley's eerie physical state, along with the new strange information from the doctors, plagued their thoughts and emotions. Every sentence they spoke was filled with hope of creating some sort of measurable change in her condition. Hope was all that was carrying them through this ordeal. Amy and Caroline said their goodbyes to Hayley, their voices filled with hope yet stifled by fear and sadness.

= *19* =

The rumbling engine of the bus provided the background music of the morning preparation for Caroline's class field trip. Her classmates lined the sidewalk near the parking lot. Chatter and laughter filled the air as the students were ready for a day away from school. Caroline sat on the rock wall near the sidewalk with her friend Dez. "What do you think we're going to be able to do today?" Caroline asked.

"I'm not sure," Dez shrugged, "They said that we're breaking into small groups and exploring the city a little before we go to dinner and the show."

"Well that should be fun," Caroline smiled, "my family never really goes to New Orleans much."

"Well we can't get into too much trouble cause we'll be stuck in groups the whole time." Dez laughed.

Caroline rolled her eyes, "Right. Cause we're definitely the troublemaking type."

"Hey you never know," Dez shrugged, "maybe I'm crazy. Maybe we're gonna bring all the voodoo back with us and take over this city."

"I don't think that's quite how it works. Although, I do agree that you're crazy" Caroline chuckled at her friend's goofy plan.

The bus door slid open and Mrs. Olivier stepped down to the sidewalk, "Alright, let's go, everyone on the bus."

Caroline hopped down off of the stone wall and picked up her backpack from the ground. "Well, time to take over the city or whatever your plan is." Caroline laughed and turned to the bus. She climbed onboard, Dez a few steps behind. The rest of the students and chaperones piled on to the bus, leaving few open spaces. The bus doors closed as the driver shifted into gear. Chatter filled the crowded bus. Dez was her usual talkative self from the moment the bus left the parking lot, talking Caroline's ear off with anything she could come up with. As quick as she had begun to ramble on and on about anything and everything, Dez turned her thoughts to Caroline's situation.

"So how is your sister doing?" She asked.

Caroline shook her head and shrugged, "I'm not really sure, they said nothing had really changed."

"Oh, I'm sorry."

"It was weird, though," Caroline explained, "They said that her mind was running wild on their tests, but her body wasn't reacting at all to it."

Dez looked on in confusion, "What the heck does that mean?"

"I don't know," said Caroline, "I don't think that they really know either. Which sucks because you can't really fix a problem without knowing what it is that you're trying to fix."

"That's for sure." Dez awkwardly fiddled with her cell phone in her lap before continuing, "You going to be alright today?"

Caroline smiled, "I'll be fine. She'll be on my mind obviously, but there isn't anything I can do to help right now so I just have to go about my day until there is something I can do."

"I hear ya. That's got to be hard, sorry if you don't want to talk about it," Dez watched as Caroline smirked while she talked, "I'm sure you don't want to keep repeating the same stuff."

Caroline lifted her head and smiled at her friend. "It's alright. You're just trying to help. Thanks, Dez. I just really wish we could get some sort of answer for all of this."

"Just keep your head up. They'll get it figured out."

"Yeah, that's what I keep telling myself." Caroline replied as the bus entered the highway toward New Orleans. The highway, bordered by water on either side, made the short trip seem much longer. Caroline found herself staring at the lake horizon for most of the ride. The bright sunny day allowed her to see for miles in either direction. Her unobstructed view provided a small amount of peace for her mind. The stillness of the open air and calm water helped Caroline keep her hope alive and level her thoughts. A small providence of peace that she desperately needed.

The shore began to appear in the distance. Caroline watched as Irish Bayou passed outside her window. The marshy landscape sprawled in every direction. Her eyes explored the deep green trees and grasses along the sides of the highway. The wild foliage grew shorter and more contained as the bus cruised from the bayous toward the city. The crisscrossing overpasses glided overhead blocking the sunshine for a brief moment. Nature soon gave way to the brick and mortar. The beautiful trees replaced with light posts and business signage.

Mrs. Olivier stood up in the front of the bus and called for attention. "Alright everyone, we're almost there. When we get to the park we will separate into our smaller groups and go our separate ways." She continued to outline the plans for the day, "You'll have until 4:30 to do whatever you would like with your groups. Please be careful and do not cause problems anywhere. Your group leader will report you to me if you do." Quiet pockets of laughter followed her veiled threat.

"There goes your voodoo plan, Dez." Caroline chuckled.

Dez laughed and snapped her fingers, "Dang, foiled again."

Mrs. Olivier gave some suggestions for possible day plans, "Feel free to go shopping or explore the city. Take in all that you can before we have to go to dinner. Just make sure you have fun today. We will all meet back here at 4:30, like I said, from here we will head to the restaurant and make our way to the theatre afterwards for the show."

The bus slowed to a halt outside French Quarter Visitor Center. The students filed off of the bus and spread out along the sidewalk. The small groups of five and six kids each joined together with their assigned chaperones. "Alright, everyone," Mrs. Olivier called out, "Make sure you are back here no later than 4:30, please." The chaperones all acknowledged her request and gathered their groups.

Mrs. Finster turned to Caroline, Dez, and the other three girls in her group looking for a plan. "Well, ladies, what should we do today?"

The girls remained mostly silent except for a few shrugs and hums of indifference. "Why don't we just explore the area?" Mrs. Finster suggested. "There are plenty of shops and stores to poke around in nearby."

"Works for me." Chimed Dez.

"I'm good with that too." Caroline replied. The other girls accepted and the group began to walk away from the bus. They made their way through Jackson Square to head into the heart of the French Quarter. The large statue of Andrew Jackson in the center of the park stood resolute amongst the well kept grass and landscaping. Saint Louis Cathedral towered over the city streets. It's immaculate white walls and grand steeples provided a picturesque backdrop to the group's march through the park. The cathedral and park combined to create a near fantasy world for Caroline. She could not help but smile at the beautiful church. It was like a princess' castle. Soon after, the cathedral was behind the girls as they continued their walk into the Quarter. Block after block the group walked, chatting and laughing while taking in the sights of the antiquated architecture and style of the neighborhoods.

Shop after shop, the girls poked around at the clothes, souvenirs, and knick knacks. Caroline and Dez goofed around with silly objects they found in the various gift shops. "Who buys this stuff?" Dez joked.

"Tourists probably," Caroline answered while pulling a gaudy bedazzled t-shirt up to her chest, "Or, you know, anyone who needs a Cajun Drinking Team shirt."

"Looks fabulous on you," Dez laughed.

The group strolled out of the shop and back on the sidewalk. Caroline looked around at the street signs and other buildings and recognized the area. "My dad lives pretty close to here." She said.

"Where?" Asked Dez.

"A few blocks from here, I think. He's working right now, though. Not like he could come see us anyway."

"Have you seen him much since he moved?"

"No," Caroline shook her head, "Hayley came here with him not too long ago to see his new place, but I wasn't able to come down that day."

"Ah, that sucks," Dez piped, "that's gotta be hard."

Caroline shrugged her shoulders, "It is, but I'm basically used to it now with how bad things had been. It was kind of a relief that the fighting had stopped with them being separated."

"I had meant to ask you about that," Dez paused, "I understand if you don't want to talk about it."

Caroline turned with a confused look, "Ask what?"

"Well, you said that your dad lived with you guys right up until your parents split."

"Right, what about it?" Caroline asked.

"How did that work?"

"I don't know. It was really weird. There was always a tension at home. He stayed because there were some hang ups with him getting a place out here and they somehow agreed to stay in the same house."

Dez nodded, "I don't know how you did it, kid. I just can't believe they agreed to that."

Caroline laughed, "I can't either. I don't know how they came to that answer. Probably had something to do with me and my sister."

"That makes sense," Dez nodded her head, "probably wanted to keep some bit of normalcy intact."

"That's really the only answer I've come up with for it."

= 20 =

Sunshine beat down on the pavement as the group followed the sidewalk. A small, seemingly out of place building, sat in between two larger businesses. The paint was dull and cracking on the small building. Its walls lacked the vibrancy and life of the surrounding area. A small second story rested above the store. It appeared to be the home of someone, most likely the owner, Caroline thought. True care and maintenance of the shop had clearly been neglected by the owner for a long time. A small wooden sign hung near the door, creaking in the light breeze. The name, Hallows of Mystery, peeked through the chipped paint of the sign. Caroline looked into the large, cloudy front window of the store as they moved closer. She could see the shape of books and some small doll-like objects on the shelves. The dirty window made it difficult to make out any discernible details of the objects.

Inside the shop looked dark and unwelcoming. Minimal light from candles and a table lamp lit the diminutive storefront. Nobody appeared to be inside although the door was wide open. "Want to go inside?" asked Dez.

Caroline shot her eyes to Dez, "Huh? I don't think so, that place is creepy."

"Oh come on, you chicken," Dez laughed, "it's just a store."

"Alright, fine." Caroline conceded and they went inside. A few of the other girls followed while the rest wandered outside. The shop smelled of old dust and grime, stagnant and dank. Old books and dolls lined the shelves of the cluttered shop. Dust lingered on the decrepit covers and book titles were obscured by their cracked leather and torn paper spines. Necklaces made of yellowed bones and teeth hung from golden hooks under the bookshelves and on the counters. Old dolls sat limp on the shelves and tables. Their eyes stared lifelessly into the distance. Caroline refrained from touching any of the dolls as she poked around the store. "I really don't like these things," she said to Dez.

Dez laughed and picked up a doll, "Why is that?"

"They're so creepy. I don't like old dolls in general but these are extra creepy."

"They're just dolls, Care. They can't do anything." Dez shook the doll at Caroline making playful ghost noises.

"Stop it," Caroline giggled and lightly pushed Dez' hand away, "you're gonna break that stupid thing."

Dez kept fiddling with the dolls on the shelves as Caroline moved back to the nearby bookshelves. With each step the floor creaked and popped under her feet. Her footsteps echoed through the hollow floor. She picked up a dusty book and began to brush the thin layer of dirt off its cover. As her hand touched the book the back door of the shop opened. The loud creaking door startled Caroline causing her to lose her grip on the book she was holding. She fumbled with the book before it fell to the table.

An old woman slowly appeared from the back room. She moved with the help of a twisted wooden cane. Her hair wrapped in a deep crimson cloth. Bright gray hair peeked out from under the wrap. Her deep ebony skin, wrinkled and worn. The clothing she wore did not fit with her urban surroundings. Her clothing dirtied and tattered like that of a old farmhand. She lifted her head toward the girls, her dark eyes squinting to focus on Caroline and Dez. "Hello children," she said in her elderly raspy tone, "welcome, welcome."

"Oh, um, hi there," Caroline nervously piped.

The woman's voice was a deep scratched tone. That of a lifelong smoker. She held an accent of a true Caribbean native. The old woman examined Caroline as she continued to poke around the shop. Caroline could feel the old woman's gaze and would glance over periodically to see her staring back at her. Feeling uncomfortable, Caroline decided to try and break the tension of the room, "So, um, how long have you had your store?"

"A long time, child. A long time." The woman answered. Her tone left a mystery without a full answer. "Since long before you were born."

Caroline, curious about the old woman, approached the counter, "So where are you from?"

"I come from Haiti," the woman answered with her heavy accent, "I come long ago with my family."

"That's very interesting. My name is Caroline, nice to meet you."

"I am Astrid." Her eyes locked with Caroline's and began to widen. "I sense sorrow in you, child."

"What... What do you mean?" Caroline was taken aback by the statement.

"Your eyes hold what your voice will not speak. You carry a heavy heart with you."

"I, well, I mean I --" Caroline stuttered out bits of a sentence.

Dez perked her head up and saw Caroline talking to Astrid and walked over to her. "You alright, Care?" She asked.

Caroline nodded, turned and whispered to Dez, "I don't know what it is but it's like this lady can see right through me."

A look of concern fell on Dez' face. "Come on, let's get you out of here."

"No," Caroline refused, "I'm not leaving yet."

Astrid continued to pull information from Caroline. "Tell me, child. Why do you hide your heart?"

"I'm not hiding anything."

"Your voice gives you away. Something is wearing on your soul," Astrid pried.

"I don't know what you're talking about." Caroline's nerves became more and more apparent. "I have my own troubles but I can't talk to you about them."

"There is something I sense in you. Something I have felt before, child. Have you a sister?"

Caroline's eyes grew larger, "I, um, I do."

"You share her aura. Your energy is the same." Astrid continued to explain and with every word, Caroline got sucked in even more, "I sense that you have been hurting for her."

"She's... She's not doing well." Caroline drooped her head.

"I feel an evil walking with your spirit." Astrid said. Caroline's heart sank at the sound of her words.

"What do you mean an evil?" Caroline shook out.

"A spirit has attached itself to your family. Your sister holds it within her. Tell me, have you seen anything strange with your sister?"

Caroline's heart was racing now. She could not believe how accurate Astrid's predictions were. She took a deep breath and revealed what happened to Hayley, "She had been acting very odd lately and tried to attack me out of nowhere one night. Now she's in the hospital."

Astrid sat silent for a moment, "She has the evil in her."

"What?" Caroline asked.

"Please, tell me, what happened before this?"

"Well," Caroline began to tell the story, "it all started when she found this old book. Ever since she had that thing, she's been acting weird."

"A book? What kind of book?" Astrid asked. Her voice got higher, as if she was surprised by Caroline's story, "Tell me about this book."

"I don't know, like a notebook," Caroline shook her head in confusion, "it was empty. It just looked like a really old diary or something. It had a lot of weird symbols on it and a big black rock on the front."

Astrid's eyes squinted in suspicion as if Caroline had struck a nerve, "Years ago, an evil spirit was released upon the earth. It preyed upon the weak and controlled their mind and body to take revenge on those who trapped it inside its gemstone prison. The spirit works very mysteriously. No one knows how it takes hold, but it is not to be trifled with."

Dez rolled her eyes and tugged on Caroline's sleeve, "Come on, let's go, this is ridiculous and I've had enough crazy for one day." Caroline slapped Dez' hand away and continued to search for information. Astrid's eyes shot daggers at Dez for her comments.

"So, what is it? Where did it come from?" Caroline sat on an old stool near the counter, her full attention held by Astrid's story.

"Nobody knows where it came from. The spirit drives its victims to madness. I have seen the effect, those afflicted are dangerous."

Caroline put her palm up to Astrid, "Wait, what do you mean dangerous?"

"The stricken become very unpredictable. They appear very ill and lose touch with their reality. When they are near the end, they cry tears of blood."

Caroline's eyes scanned the room in shock at what she was hearing, "How do you know so much about the spirit?" Caroline asked.

Astrid awkwardly paused and looked around the room, "Tales of the spirit have been passed on for generations. Tales of the weak being used for spiritual vengeance have existed for centuries. People have tried to control the spirit for ages."

"So is this like voodoo or something?"

"No no," Astrid wagged her finger, "this is not voodoo. This is stronger than any other spirit I have known. Its origin remains a mystery. The strong are not taken by it."

"What do you mean the weak and strong?"

"Only the weak of will succumb to the deeds of evil. Life is earned by those who refuse to fade into the darkness. Evil is a scavenger, and to it, a heart full of life is untouchable. The evil often is far too strong for anyone to handle and they are driven to death."

Caroline became visibly flustered, "I know this sounds crazy but is it possible my sister could be possessed?" Possessed. The word came crashing out of her mouth like an avalanche.

"The gemstone holding the spirit was stolen years ago. I," Astrid paused again as if she was choosing her words carefully, "I don't know where it could be now."

Caroline glared at Astrid, "Don't lie to me."

"You watch your tongue, child." Astrid pointed at Caroline, "I do not know where the stone is. I can only feel that it is near and that it's power is growing. That someone is under its control."

Caroline's breathing grew quicker, "How close?"

"Very close. I have felt the spirit's presence. I have seen it before. I know what it does. The taken are prisoners within their own body. Slaves to a master that they cannot see. They are built stronger and stronger as a vessel for the spirit. It must be trapped again before it is too late. A cursed victim is often chosen by a practitioner of the spirit because of their perceived inner strength. Few know how to curse a victim, fewer know how to control one."

"How can someone curse another person?" Caroline asked, "And how can it be controlled?"

"It is not that simple. The process of each is very complex and can only be done by those who have years and years of knowledge of this scourge. Driving the spirit gives full control of the afflicted."

Caroline looked around the store and saw that her group had already left. Soon after, her phone vibrated in her pocket.

Caroline was not ready to leave without finding out more information about this curse. "How can it be fixed?"

"I have been told of one ritual that could possibly return the spirit to its stone, but could possibly release it again, however the possessed would need to be brought to me," Astrid explained, "it is a very intense and dangerous sacrament."

"Are you," she paused, "are you able to control the demon?"

"Just what exactly are you getting at, little girl?" Astrid's tone changed from gentle to annoyed and angered with Caroline's question.

"You seem to know an awful lot about this demon. I think you're hiding something about it." Caroline accusatory tone did not sit well with Astrid.

"Go. You must leave now," Astrid commanded, "You are no longer welcome here."

"You are lying," Caroline snapped and pounded her hand on the counter, "I know it. You know more than you're telling me."

Astrid slammed her hand on the counter, "Leave. Now! You little rat. The evil will find you sooner than you know."

"Tell me!" Caroline shouted.

"Get out," Astrid grumbled, "The evil will always bring you back."

Caroline shook her head and stormed out of the store. "Stupid old hag," she said to herself, "I'll prove it." Looking up and down the street she couldn't find her group. She then remembered that she received a text while in the store. The text message was from Dez, "We're across the street at the record shop."

= *21* =

Caroline caught up to the group inside the record store. "How were things in the loony bin?" Dez joked.

"Don't start," Caroline snipped, "that woman is mean. She flipped out at me and kicked me out for asking if she could summon some demon she was talking about."

"She's just a crazy old woman. All the nonsense in her store has gone to her head."

"You're probably right," Caroline flipped through some old records to her left and paused, "It's just, just that everything she was talking about was so spot on with what's been going on."

"Care, anyone could have done that. Look, your sister is in the hospital, she's not well. She's not herself, did creepy stuff, it was scary. See, I can do it too."

"Yeah, I guess so. I think I just want answers so bad that I actually want to believe her." Caroline nodded, "Thanks, Dez."

"She's just like those stupid T.V. psychics. They find someone, ask some vague questions, and there you have it, 'answers' or whatever."

"True. Well I fell dumb now." Caroline chuckled and shook her head. She went back to thumbing through the records as her thoughts wandered. Thoughts of her rough experience with the awful woman in the previous shop ran through her head. Caroline felt sick to her stomach from Astrid's attitude and apparent lies. She refused to believe that Astrid's knowledge was limited to what was told. "Why would she freak out at me for asking if she could call the demon?" Caroline questioned out loud while looking the record crates.

Dez flung her head toward the ceiling, "Seriously? Caroline, let it go, girl. She's a wacko, just forget her nonsense."

"I can't just forget it, Dez. What if she's telling the truth?" Caroline dropped the records back into place, "What if she really can fix it?"

"Let's just act, for a minute, like she's not a crazy person and she actually is who she says she is. What if her doing her little ritual makes it worse? Or kills your sister? What then?"

Caroline angrily shook her head at Dez' harsh scenario, "Don't you even talk about that."

"It's the truth, Caroline. She might just make everything worse than it is. I wouldn't rush to bring your sick sister to some random person just because they say that they can fix it."

"Alright, sorry. I'll try to stop thinking about it."

"Good," Dez bounced her head, "now let's go. I think we're heading to meet up with another group now." She placed the records she was looking at back upon the shelf as Mrs. Finster called out the group, "Let's go, ladies. Time to head back to the bus."

The bell on the shop door rang repeatedly as the group of girls made their way out of the shop and back out into the hot New Orleans' sun. Caroline was unable to keep her eyes focused ahead as her thoughts remained on the vile woman in the old bookstore. She walked alongside Dez as she watched the cars pass them on the street. Saint Louis Cathedral could be seen in the distance, its steeple peeked over the rooftops of the city.

The well groomed grounds of Jackson Square were soon upon them. Mrs. Finster directed the girls through the park and back to the lot on the other side. The rumbling bus engine could be heard in the distance. One by one the girls filed back onto the bus, greeting the other students that had gotten back before them. Quiet chatter grew louder and louder until Mrs. Olivier had to step in and quiet the kids back down. After a quick headcount, the bus pulled away from the lot toward the restaurant.

A short bus ride later, the students arrived at the restaurant for dinner. They left the bus, entered, and took their seats. Dez took her place next to Caroline, as always. Caroline eyes quickly scanned the room, looking around the room at the vintage artwork and decor. Dez noticed that Caroline was not being herself anymore. "What's up, kid?" Caroline remained silent. "Hey, Caroline," Dez gave her a light slap on the shoulder, "still with us?"

"Huh? Nothing. I'm fine." Caroline responded tersely.

"Is this still about the voodoo women? Just relax, man."

"I just feel like she's right, ya know?" Caroline explained, "she was basically right about everything that has happened with my sister."

Dez tapped and twirled her fork on the table, "Don't get too caught up in that. She's just some random stranger spewing out nonsense."

"Yeah, but what if she's not? What if she really is right?" Caroline asked.

"Well, I don't know what you would do then." Dez replied.

"Me either, and that's what I'm afraid of." Caroline anxiously crushed her napkin in her hand, her nerves wreaking havoc in her stomach.

The group continued to chat and laugh together until their food arrived. Caroline remained fairly quiet throughout, only responding periodically to her friends. She kept her head low while she slowly picked at her wrap. Waiters popped in and out of the group's room removing plates as necessary. Caroline lifted her head as Mrs. Olivier called for everyone to start getting ready to leave. She chomped down large bites as quickly as she could as the group got up to leave. Dez laughed at Caroline's bulging cheeks and received a smack on the arm. The group spilled out of the restaurant and back onto the bus. Caroline found her seat as the bus pulled away from the restaurant.

The bright lights of the Saenger Theatre shined above the streets in the distance. All of the students exited on the sidewalk near the entrance of the theater. Mrs. Olivier moved to the head of the group and led them inside. Beautiful chandeliers lit the foyer leading to the lobby. Caroline looked around at the high ceilings and sophisticated architecture. Golden stone walls and framed posters of upcoming opera and theater shows lined the way to the main lobby. The floor was made of a grid of polished stone tiles. Walking into the main lobby the group was greeted by large drink bar. Saenger Theatre branded carpet covered the floor and colorful, intricately designed ceilings rested overhead. The group climbed the stairs to the second level of the theater.

Entering the main auditorium felt like walking into an entire new world. The soft red seats sat in the center of the auditorium. The whole room was designed and built to look like an outdoor theater. The deep blue ceiling featured small lights throughout to simulate a peaceful night sky. Ancient Greek style statues sat on the roofs of the outlying buildings. Caroline examined the statues from her seat, almost lifelike in their appearance. The lights in the theater began to dim and music began to play. Caroline looked toward the stage but could still see the dimly lit statues to her right.

Caroline caught a flutter of motion out of the corner of her eye and looked toward the statues. She found that nothing was moving when she looked to the dark rooftop. Looking back to the stage she saw motion in her peripheral vision again, although, she again saw nothing when she peeked toward the statues. Caroline slowly turned her gaze back toward the stage but stopped and peered back again. She ignored the action on stage and stared at the statue nearest to her, waiting for it to move again. The face of the statue began to contort. Ivory stone cracked and split as the neck turned and mouth opened. Its eyes spilled blood down its stone cheeks and smoke seeped from its mouth. The blood, nearly black in color, poured down the statue's face and down its neck. Caroline stared in horror as the ivory figure's jaw dropped nearly twice as far as possible by a human and the cloud of ebony smoke wafted out. Her breathing raced as she pulled her legs up to her chest and covered her eyes with her hands. Dez felt a bump on her arm and heard a quiet whimper from Caroline. She looked over to see Caroline trying her best to hide her vision from the atrocity.

"Hey," Dez whispered in confusion, "what are you doing?"

Caroline lifted her head toward Dez, "What? Umm, nothing."

"What's the matter?"

"Nothing." Caroline curtly answered and looked away. Dez rolled her eyes and returned to watching the show.

Caroline slowly looked back toward the statue. The marble carving sat inanimate with no visible signs of the blood that had been pouring out of it. Its face and pose had returned to its original stoic state. Caroline's watched the actors dance and sing on stage yet her attention was still held by the statues on the wall. Peering over every few minutes, Caroline found that the stone figures remained motionless. No signs of change were evident on any statue. The cracking body and stained face had completely disappeared as if they were never there.

The show's intermission came shortly after. The group stood up from their seats and filed onto the concourse. Caroline walked away from the rest of the group and paced about the crowded room while she tried to clear the thoughts from her mind. She ran her hand along the smooth walls and watched the other people mill about. Caroline felt a sharp burning pain in her left forearm. She quickly dropped her hand from the wall and examined her arm. A scar was appearing in her skin right before her eyes, As if an invisible blade was slicing through her skin. Her eyes widened at the frightful sight. The stinging pain would not subside as the scar continued to grow. Caroline covered the mark with her hand to hide it from the people in the crowd. Her fingertips felt the strange mark expand while she covered it. People continued to move around her, unaware of her situation. She began to walk toward the restroom on the other end of the lobby.

Dez saw Caroline walking alone around the room and worked through the crowd over to her. She came up behind Caroline and tapped her on the shoulder, causing Caroline to jump. "What's going on with you? Why are you acting so goofy?" She asked.

"I'm not." Caroline said, immediately looking away from Dez.

"Seriously?" Dez laughed, "You've been acting weird ever since that crazy old hag was talking to you."

"I'm fine. Just distracted today."

"Is that why you were acting like a scared puppy during the show?" Dez questioned.

"I-I-" Caroline stuttered, "I just got startled by something, that's all."

"By what?" asked Dez.

"I don't want to talk about it, alright?" Caroline snapped.

"Whatever. Just get it together, kid. You're starting to freak me out."

"I'll be fine. I need to go to the bathroom. I'll meet you back inside." Caroline said as she peeled away from Dez and walked to the restroom.

Caroline quickly took the only open stall remaining and locked the door. She checked her arm and found that the scar had ceased growing. The puffy pink skin had already begun to dry and flake yet was still very sensitive to touch. The lights of the restroom dimmed and rose again to signal the shows restart and Caroline left the restroom.

The audience funneled back to their seats after the intermission. Caroline's eyes were locked on the statues as she walked back to her seat. Her fear began to subside seeing that the statues remained lifeless. She was starting to think that she was just seeing things and scared herself. "Statues can't come to life," she mumbled to herself, "get it together, C." The play continued without a hitch. Caroline watched the remainder of the show without fearing the figures along the walls.

Mrs. Olivier waited at the top of the stairs to direct the group out into the lobby. They filed out of the theater and back onto the bus. Caroline kept quiet and to herself on the walk back to the bus. She took a seat next to the window and quietly watched the passing buildings. The lights of the theater marquee faded in the distance as the bus drove farther and farther away.

The drive through the downtown traffic took longer than expected. Stop and go traffic from the theater delayed the group's return home. Caroline watched the bright city lights go by her window. Soon her view grew much darker as the highway pulled away from New Orleans and over the bridge back to Eden Isle. The highway grew darker and darker with the dwindling city lights along the road over the lake. Caroline stared into the distance, nothing was visible outside of the highway. The dark of the night had fully engulfed the horizon. Her mind returned to thoughts of her sister, thoughts of hope.

= 22 =

Dez dropped Caroline off at home after the trip. Stars had begun to peek through the lightly cloud covered sky overhead. The humidity of the day had lifted after the sun fell. Caroline grabbed her bag and got out of Dez' car. "Hey," called Dez and Caroline turned back toward the car, "keep me posted, alright?"

"I will. Thanks, Dez." Caroline smiled and patted her hand on the top of the car door. She walked to the garage and entered the code to open the door. As it opened she wondered to herself if anything had changed with her sister's condition. Caroline opened the door to the house and found her mother sitting and reading in the living room.

"Hey sweety," Amy greeted, "how was your trip?"

"It was fun," Caroline paused, debating to tell her mother about the strange curio shop incident during her trip, "we just walked around the city for a while, went to dinner, and then went to the show."

"See anything cool in the city?" Amy asked.

"I liked the old buildings. It's cool to see all of them." Caroline took a seat in the chair across from her mother.

"Did Dez give you a ride home tonight?"

"Yeah she did."

"How is she doing?" Amy asked.

"Oh she's fine," Caroline replied, "not really doing anything special."

"So did you get anything from any of the shops?"

Caroline shook her head, "No. Nothing really caught my eye today."

"It happens," Amy shrugged.

"We went into a kind of knick knack, voodoo type shop before dinner. It was really strange. The woman there was--" Caroline started to explain but drifted off before she spoke too much about her aggressive exchange with Astrid.

"Was what?" Amy questioned.

"Well, um, weird, she was just really weird."

"That's not really surprising though, is it?" Amy chuckled, "If it was a strange kind of store then I'd assume the owner would be a bit out there."

"Yeah, I guess so." Caroline fiddled with the seam of the chair arm. She looked around the room until her mother spoke up again.

"So what was so strange about this woman?"

"She was just kind of creepy all over," Caroline explained, "she looks like she's straight out of a scary movie. The stuff in her store just made her seem even creepier."

"Well it probably helps business to have a bit of mystery in the store." Amy set the book she was holding on the end table, "I stopped to see your sister today."

Caroline perked her head up, "So what did you find out?"

Amy shrugged her shoulders, "Nothing new really. They told me that her breathing had shifted from the last couple days."

"So what does that mean? Shifted how?" Caroline asked.

"I didn't know what they meant either, but when we went to check on her I could tell," Amy turned more directly toward Caroline, "you know when you have a cold and sometimes you wheeze and your breathing sounds kind of scratchy?"

"Yeah," Caroline answered, "is that what she sounds like?"

"Kind of. She sort of sounds like she's growling sometimes."

Caroline gave her mother a confused glance, "So is that a bad sign or what?"

"They told me that it doesn't appear to be a problem. Just keeping us posted on her condition."

"What is her condition exactly?" Caroline asked her mother.

Amy shook her head in frustration at the question, "Still don't know, sweety. I wish we did. We'll go see her tomorrow after breakfast, though."

"Good. I need to see her again," Caroline felt her eyes begin to well with tears but forced herself to hold them in, "I need my sister back."

"Don't worry, sweetheart. Everything is going to be alright." Amy comforted her daughter and picked up her book again, "Just go and try to get some rest tonight and we'll be with her again in no time."

"Okay, Mom. I'll try." Caroline got up from her chair and walked upstairs to her room. She flicked the light switch near her door and stood in the doorway. The lavender bed sat directly in front of her, its white metal headboard rested against the wall she shared with her sister. She flung her bag into the side of the bed and climbed onto the mattress. She stared at the ceiling and watched the fan. Following the blades as they spun over and over. Letting out a sigh she closed her eyes and began to pray, "Please God," she whispered, "if you're there, please help my sister Hayley. She needs your help so badly right now. I'm so scared for her and that I may never see the real her again." Tears began to seep from her eyes and roll down the sides of her face. "She is so much stronger than anyone knows. Please help her, please. Please help."

She rubbed her upper arm to try and calm herself. Her hand slid down to her forearm and she noticed that she could not feel the scar anymore. Quickly she glanced to the spot it appeared. Her skin was as smooth as it was before the scar appeared. She felt her other arm and noticed that the first scar had also disappeared, though she didn't know when. Her disbelief at the now missing marks was only surpassed by her relief. She cracked a small alleviated smile and rolled onto her side. She grabbed her phone from her bag and sent Dez a message to update her about Hayley's condition. Caroline set her phone on her nightstand, closed her eyes, and slowly drifted to sleep.

"Wake up, kiddo," Amy shook Caroline's shoulder, "it's time to go."

Caroline rolled over to face her mother and rubbed the sleep from her eyes, "Okay, I'll be out in a minute," she softly mumbled.

"I'll be downstairs when you're ready."

Caroline sat up in her bed, letting out a long yawn. The sunlight lit up her room while she rose to get dressed. She grabbed a tank top and shorts from her dresser drawers. After getting ready for the day she stood in front of the mirror, looking at her outfit. She looked at the reflection of her arms, smiling at the now missing burns. Caroline grabbed her phone off of her nightstand and slipped it into her pocket before walking downstairs.

Amy stood up from the kitchen table when Caroline came down the stairs. "All set?" she asked.

"Yeah, I'm ready." Caroline answered.

"Let's go then." Amy pulled her keys off of the hook near the door and they left the house into the Louisiana morning heat.

= *23* =

"You ready?" Amy asked, turning the engine off. She looked toward her daughter and gave her a comforting smile.

Caroline returned a shy half smile to her mother, "I guess so, I don't even know what to expect anymore." The hospital entryway was quiet on this morning. Only a couple people milled about the doorway, some talking on cell phones, one reading the morning paper. Sunlight reflected off of the hospital windows and directly into Caroline's eyes as she turned away from the car. She squinted and shielded her eyes from the light and tilted her head down out of the glare. Her eyes were able to readjust after entering the hospital lobby.

Caroline and her mother checked in at the desk and walked to Hayley's room. The lobby was quiet and mostly empty. A small family sat in the waiting area, chatting together quietly. Caroline watched the nurses and other workers coming in and out of the lobby as they went about their business. As they walked to the room a door opened behind them and a voice called out.

"Hi there, Amy." Meredith waved as she closed the door.

"Oh hello, Meredith." Amy greeted her as they walked into Hayley's room.

Caroline opened the door and stepped into Hayley's room. "Dad!" she gasped and ran to her father, immediately wrapping her arms around him as tightly as she could.

"Hi, sweetheart," Eli greeted, "it's so nice to see you again."

"Eli." Amy nodded.

Eli lifted his head to the sound of his name, "Hello, Amy." He turned his gaze to Hayley, "How is she doing now?"

"Same as she has been for the last couple days as far as I know."

"I was afraid of that." He quietly answered.

Caroline looked to her father, "Where have you been, Dad? How come you haven't been here?"

"I have been, Caroline." He gestured his hand toward Amy, "Your mom tried to call me that night but I didn't have my phone on while I was sleeping. So she called me the morning after Hayley came here. I've come during the day every day since."

"Oh," Caroline looked confused, "Why didn't you tell me he had been coming, Mom?"

"You were busy in school. I didn't need to add to your distractions by telling you your dad would be in town again."

"Yeah, but--" Caroline tried to interject.

"And," Amy cut her daughter off, "I knew he would be here this morning and that you'd be able to see him now."

"I've been checking with your mom periodically while I haven't been here."

"Oh, well at least we're all here now." Caroline said with a smile.

A small knock could be heard on the door as it slowly opened. A moment later Meredith's head poked around the door. "Hi, everyone," she quietly acknowledged, walking over to Hayley's bed she swiftly glanced over the machines and their provided information.

"How is she doing today, Meredith?" Amy asked.

"Well," Meredith answered while checking the monitors, "her levels all seem to be consistent with the last few days. Apart from her breathing changing, I'd have to say that still nothing has changed."

"Oh right," Amy piped, "I meant to ask you about that. What do you think happened with her breathing?"

"Hard to say, really. Could be her lungs trying to clear a little bit, could be a kind of narrowing in her airway similar to snoring, it doesn't have a concrete answer yet."

"I'm so tired of not having any answers." Caroline huffed, visibly frustrated.

"I know, sweety. We all are." Amy tried to calm her daughter.

"Hayley's a very peculiar case," Meredith chimed in, "nothing has changed that we can detect, but apart from her being unconscious, nothing hints at anything being wrong with her."

"So why isn't she awake?" Asked Eli.

"Unfortunately, no one knows." Meredith added, "I'm very sorry that this has been so stressful for all of you. I promise that we're working very hard to find a remedy for Hayley's condition."

She flipped through her clipboard and wrote a couple notes. Meredith walked back out of the room after checking the remaining levels. Eli paced around the front of the room mumbling to himself. He looked to his family with a heavy heart. "We have to get this figured out," he whispered in his slight southern drawl while shaking his head. He took a seat at the corner of Hayley's bed, "we just have to."

Caroline walked to the window and turned the chair away to face out over the parking lot. She sulked in the chair, placing her hands over her face. Amy looked to her daughter and saw the sadness surrounding her. She walked to her and took the seat to the right. Amy placed her hand on Caroline's back, "Everything will be alright, sweetheart. Try to keep your head up."

"How can I?" Caroline pleaded, "Nothing is changing. How can I keep my head up when all I see, day in and day out, is my sister lying in a bed, dead to the world?"

Amy lowered her head, "I know it's hard, Caroline. Your sister is stronger than you think. She'll pull through this and everything will be back to normal soon."

"But when, Mom? It's been days." Caroline's eyes began to burn with tears and her voice started to shake. "I can't lose my sister, Mom. I can't. I don't know what I would do without her."

Amy too began to feel a lump in her throat at her daughter's emotional pleas. "Don't think that way. You are not going to lose your sister, I promise. Please try to keep your head up. You've got to try to keep going with your everyday life."

"I'm trying, I really am. It's all so sudden, I just can't get it out of my head."

"I can't either, Caroline. You'll never get it out until it's over." She rubbed her daughter's back, "Just know that everything is going to get better. We're all going to get through this together."

"I believe you. I just don't know what to do until that time."

"This will all be over before you know it, dear." Amy looked to Hayley and wiped her eyes. "She's going to be okay."

Caroline slid her chair over to Hayley's side and placed her hand on her sister's hand. Hayley's skin felt cold to Caroline's touch. Caroline's heart dropped due to the lifeless feeling hand she was holding. "This doesn't even feel real," she said to her mother, "she feels so cold, like she's not a real person."

"She's still in there. The doctors are going to get this all figured out and she'll be back to normal in no time." Amy shifted her chair beside the bed as well. "We're all hurting more than we show, Care."

"I know, Mom." Caroline nodded.

"Your sister is a fighter," Eli chimed in, "she is going to get through this." The sun shined through the window, making a bright glare from the floor and onto Hayley's bed. The light illuminated Hayley like she had been chosen by the angels. Caroline felt the light warming her hands and Hayley's cool body. It brought a small feeling of relaxation and comfort back to Caroline's heart. Quiet came over the room as they all looked upon Hayley.

"We should get going so the doctors can keep working." Eli suggested.

Caroline nodded and squeezed Hayley's hand, "We're going to go now Hay. Everything is going to be okay. I promise." Amy smiled at her daughter's thoughtful words.

"I agree," said Amy, "come on, Caroline. Let's go get our shopping done. The three of them marched back into the lobby and past Meredith as she was working at the nurse's station.

"I'll keep you updated on Hayley." Meredith called to the family.

"Thank you, Meredith."

The family walked out of the hospital and back into the mid-morning sun. Caroline walked in between both of her parents. The weather was stifling this day, sticky and sweltering. A storm would likely follow and break the humidity. Caroline stuck her tongue out and gave a disgusted grunt at the unpleasant weather. Eli turned toward his truck and nodded to Amy, "Let me know if you hear anything."

"Of course. I'll keep you posted." Amy answered.

"Bye, Dad." Caroline waved to her father and he turned and returned a wave. Eli climbed into his truck and drove out of sight.

= *24* =

Caroline and her mother walked from shop to shop, poking around and trying on clothes. The remainder of the morning quickly faded into the early afternoon as they tried on outfits and sampled perfumes and lotions. Caroline enjoyed these rare alone times with her mom as Hayley did not like to shop the same way they did. She preferred to be in and out of stores as quickly as she could.

Caroline bought a few small charms for Hayley, a heart, a silver star, and a golden phoenix. She planned to add the charms to Hayley's bracelet that she kept on her desk in her room. "She'll like those." Amy said, smiling at her daughter.

"I think so," Caroline said, "she's always had a thing for phoenixes."

"Yes she has. I've noticed the not so subtle one in her room." Amy quipped while rolling her eyes.

Caroline chuckled, "Yeah, she's very proud of that one."

"You know her very well don't you?" Amy asked.

"As well as she'll let me," Caroline shrugged, "She's kind of private about a lot of things. She hasn't always been like that."

"That she is. I miss--" Amy's phone rang, interrupting her mid-sentence. She grabbed the phone from her purse and recognized the number of the hospital calling. Her heart began to race with anxiety.

"Hello," she answered, "this is Amy."

"Hello, Amy. This is Meredith from Hearthstone." Meredith's voice shook as if she was very nervous.

"Hi, Meredith. Is everything alright?"

"Um, not exactly."

"Meredith. What's wrong?" Amy began to feel a lump in her throat as her nerves took over, "Please tell me Hayley is okay." She pleaded. Caroline looked to her mother, feeling nauseated. Amy walked out of the store, Caroline followed close behind.

"She has, I don't really know how to say this. She has, um, gone missing." Meredith stuttered out the horrible news.

"What?!" Amy shouted, her bag falling to the floor. Caroline flinched at her mother's sudden outburst. "What do mean she's missing, Meredith?"

"Please try to stay calm, Amy. We're doing everything we can to find her."

"How do you expect me to do that? How did this happen?" Amy yelled.

"We checked up on her, saw no changes, so we left her room. When we came back after an hour or so, she was gone," Meredith explained, "I'm so sorry. She showed no signs of being alert enough to move at all."

"I can't believe that this could happen. Not in any way. I, I--"

Meredith interrupted, "We have people scouring the entire hospital for her. There is no way that she could have gotten far."

Tears began to run down Amy's face, "I'm on my way." She hung up the phone and forcefully shoved it back into her purse. "Let's go, Caroline. Now."

"What's wrong, Mom?" She asked, fearing the worst.

"I don't know how, but your sister went missing. Missing. At a hospital. How in the world does that happen?"

"Please tell me you're joking." Caroline begged.

"I wish I was. This is absurd." Amy and Caroline ran back to the car. Amy slammed her door and turned on the engine. Speeding out of the parking lot, she recklessly turned back on to the main road. She weaved in and out of the afternoon traffic as fast as she was able to.

"Mom, please be careful. You're driving crazy right now."

"Caroline, stop it. Not the time."

"Sorry." Caroline dropped her head. She turned to look out the window. Cars and buildings passed in a blur as Amy sped down the streets.

"Someone better have some real answers for me when we get there." Amy gripped the steering wheel so hard that her knuckles turned white. She clinched and ground her teeth while driving. Her anger was more visible and frightening than Caroline had seen in years. "How does something like this happen? Honestly." Amy continued to vent her frustrations. "It's a God damn hospital. How does someone just disappear?"

"I don't know, Mom. I'm as worried and confused as you are."

"I am so furious right now. This is so unacceptable. How do you lose someone's child? How do you do that?"

"I don't know. It doesn't make any sense at all." Caroline firmly gripped the door during the drag race back to the hospital.

"No!" Amy shouted as the traffic signal ahead turned red. Smacking her hand against the steering wheel she soundly stepped on the brakes. "Come on, come on." She pleaded, waiting and waiting as cars crossed through the intersection. Caroline impatiently tapped her fingers on the open window. Amy wrenched her hands tighter on the wheel. She restlessly let out frustrated forceful breath after breath. The passing cars began to slow with their own signal changing. Amy sat more upright prepping for her light to turn. "Go!" She barked at the cars in front of her. She punched the gas as soon as the traffic began to move. Taking any open space she could, Amy weaved around the other cars on the road. The hospital roof peeked over the tops of the other buildings on the block. Amy stopped the car harshly in the hospital parking lot. She slammed the door and ran across the lot through the emergency room entrance. Caroline again followed closely behind.

"Meredith?" Amy called out as she ran to the desk. "Where is Meredith?" she asked the nurse at the station.

"I don't know, ma'am. I can page her for you." The nurse answered.

"Please do, right now. It's an emergency. This hospital lost my daughter. How does that happen?"

"Oh my God." The nurse said, lifting her hand to her mouth. "I will page hers immediately." As soon as the nurse finished her sentence Amy heard running footsteps coming from around the corner to her right. Meredith came jogging around the corner.

"Amy." she gasped.

"Meredith. What's going on? Where is she?"

"We're looking as fast as we can. I promise you that," Meredith continued explaining while catching her breath, "I want to show you something we found in her room."

"Why?" Caroline asked, "We have to keep looking."

"We're going to. You both need to see this first." Meredith said, carrying a dark tone in her voice.

"What is it, Meredith?" Amy asked.

"Come with me, we'll go right now." Meredith led the two of them back to Hayley's hospital room. She walked over to Hayley's bed and pointed to the pillow at the head of the bed.

Amy's eyes widened at the sight of the pillow, "What is that?" she sternly asked, staring at the small crimson stains trailing off the edge of the pillow and bed.

"It's blood. No doubt." Meredith answered.

"Blood? How?" Amy asked. Caroline stood in shock at Meredith's news.

"That's where we hit a block, it doesn't make sense. She had no wounds."

"So," Amy paused, confused by the new discovery, "how did she start bleeding?"

"I didn't want to bring this up before with the doctors around, but I-"

"But what?" Amy interrupted, looking back to study the stains.

"I'm beginning to think that this may not be a medical issue." Meredith said and grabbed her necklace. A small golden crucifix hung around her neck on a short chain. She nervously rubbed the cross in between her thumb and index finger.

"What does 'not a medical issue' mean?" Amy asked. Her voice full of nerves and concern.

"I mean that I think there could be something darker involved with this," Meredith whispered, "something not human."

Amy's face turned stoic, feeling she was being strung along, "Meredith. Do you mean to tell me you think that is caused by aliens or something?"

Caroline chirped in, "Mom, I think she means that it could be a demon."

Meredith nodded and lightly bit her lower lip. "It finally hit me last night. Why none of the tests figured anything out. Why none of the treatments worked."

"A demon? Seriously?" Amy skeptically questioned.

"I know it sounds impossible to believe, but every story I have ever heard about something like this has gone the same way." Meredith moved to the foot of Hayley's bed, leaned on the edge, and continued to explain, "No one could figure out what was going on until it was too late. I just think that we can't rule this out. I don't want it to be too late for Hayley."

Amy began to get choked up at the thought of losing her daughter. "Alright," she conceded, "what do we have to do?"

"We have to find her." Meredith answered, "Then get her to the right kind of help. The hospital can't do anything about it."

Caroline stood stunned next to the bed. The color drained from her face and her eyes opened wide in astonishment, "Oh my god," she whispered, "She was right."

"What?" Amy turned to her daughter. "What did you say?"

Caroline paused for a moment, her shock holding her tongue captive, "That creepy old woman in New Orleans. The one in the store I told you about."

"What did she say?" Amy asked. Meredith rose off of the bed and gave her full attention to Caroline.

Caroline shook her head in confusion and began to tell the story of her encounter with Astrid. "It can't be. She said that she could tell that Hayley had the evil inside of her."

"The evil?" Amy asked.

"Yeah, like there's something inside her that's controlling her. She said that she had seen the evil before and that some gem thing had been stolen from her a long time ago. She told me that there was a demon that was trapped in it before. A really bad one."

Meredith moved closer to Caroline, "Did she say anything else?"

Caroline nodded, "I kept asking her about this stuff cause she seemed to know a lot about it. She said that she had known of a ritual that could reverse the curse, but I don't know if this is the thing she was talking about."

"Sounds like we know where to go." Meredith chimed in.

Amy put her hand up to get the others' attention, "How do we know she wasn't just making things up?"

"I don't know," Caroline answered, "but I kept asking her how she knew so much about this and I felt like she was hiding something. Then I kind of accused her of hiding things and she freaked out and yelled at me and told me to leave."

"That does sound pretty shady." Meredith added, "I think it's something to look into. Maybe we need to talk to her."

Caroline shook her head in disagreement, "I don't think she's just going to give up all her information, but she's definitely hiding something."

"She might be dangerous if she really does know about rituals like that. I wouldn't go alone if I were you." Meredith warned.

"Believe me, I'm not going back to see that woman unless I have absolutely have to. No question."

Amy sternly spoke up. "That's enough. Regardless of whatever this woman can or can't do, we can't just sit here talking about doing something. We have to find Hayley."

"I agree," said Caroline, "let's go."

"Meredith, you keep searching around here," Amy ordered, "we'll look in the surrounding area."

"Got it. Good luck." Meredith answered.

"You too." Caroline replied as Meredith darted away and ran up the hallway away from Hayley's room. Amy and Caroline quickly left the room and swiftly clipped out of the hospital. Caroline pulled her cell phone from her pocket before giving her mother her plan. "Okay, so I'm going to call Devin and get him to pick me up and help look. I'll have Dez start looking too. You call

Dad and anyone else you can think of and we'll all look around town. Call the police too if you have to."

Amy nodded her head at Caroline's plan, "Good idea. Let's do that."

"Devin and I will look around this area, you go back towards home and look."

"Alright. Keep me posted." Amy left to go to her car and drove away from the hospital. Caroline walked up and down the sidewalk outside of the emergency room entrance. She called Dez, telling her to start looking for Hayley. Dez promised to start looking near her house right away. Dez's home was on the opposite end of town from Caroline and Hayley's and would help spread the search farther.

She dialed Devin's number but received no answer. She hung up and tried again. Again no answer. "Come on, come on. Please answer me." She nervously muttered to herself. Her heart began to beat faster, her nerves rising. Devin was a necessity for this. She figured his strength might be of crucial assistance if they were able to find her. Caroline was not strong enough to handle her older sister on her own. One more try. The phone rang. Once. Twice. A third time. Click.

"Hello?" Devin answered, his voice groggy as if he had just woken up.

"Devin!" Caroline exclaimed, "I need your help, it's an emergency."

"What's going on?" He asked.

"Hayley is missing from the hospital. We don't have any idea where she is."

"What?" His voice dropped, clearly uneasy, "Oh man that's crazy. What do you need me to do?" He questioned.

"Come pick me up at the hospital right now, please." Caroline requested, "We'll start looking from here."

"Of course, I'm on my way. I'll be there soon."

"Thank you so much." Caroline hung up, nearly dropping her phone because her hands were shaking so fiercely. She anxiously paced the sidewalk waiting for Devin to arrive.

= 25 =

Caroline's heavy anxiety was partially lifted at the sight of Devin's truck hastily pulling into the hospital parking lot. His windows halfway down and his music could be heard from where Caroline was standing. She darted from the sidewalk and climbed into the pickup. Devin turned down the loud music after Caroline took her seat. His hair still tossed and messy from lying in bed. The dark sunglasses he was wearing hid his brown eyes from view. He rhythmically tapped his fingers on his steering wheel. The bright daylight began to fade as clouds began to roll across the sky. Dark clouds could be seen in the far distance. "Thank you so much for coming. I got so worried when I couldn't get a hold of you." Caroline piped and closed the door.

"Yeah sorry, I fell asleep after going to the gym. So what happened?" Devin asked.

"They called my mom while we were out shopping and said that Hayley had gone missing and that no one knew where she was."

"Wait, so no one saw her, like, get up and just walk out?" Devin asked, clearly confused, "She's been unconscious for days. How does no one see that person leave?"

"I don't know. We need to get going though." Caroline demanded.

"Got it. Where are we going to start looking?" Devin asked as he drove his truck out of the parking lot.

"I'm not really sure. I told my mom we would just look around this area of town, so I guess let's just start driving around the blocks." Caroline pulled her hair back into a ponytail, rolled the window all the way down, and hung her arm out.

"I can't imagine she got very far, yeah?" Devin asked.

"I'd doubt it." Caroline shrugged, "Don't know how she could after being out for so long."

"Right? She has to be beyond weak now." said Devin, scanning the streets for Hayley. He examined every passing person as they drove by them. No luck spying Hayley. Caroline hung her head out of the window, periodically calling out her sister's name. No one responded to her calls apart from a few puzzled looks from the passing pedestrians. Street by street they searched frantically for Hayley for forty-five minutes. There were no signs of anything out of the ordinary on any road they searched.

Devin pulled the truck to the side of the road and turned off the engine. Caroline looked to him, her eyebrow furrowed, "What are you doing? We have to keep looking." She forcefully gestured her hand toward the street.

"We've been looking for almost an hour. We have to start being more direct with our plan."

"What are you talking about?" Caroline asked.

"I mean we have to take this on foot, start asking people, looking in stores." He unbuckled his seatbelt and placed his hand on the door handle, "It's really unlikely that we'll just see her on the street. We might be too fast in my car to see everything we need to. I can't look for Hayley that well if I have to keep an eye on the road too."

Caroline bounced her head, "Yeah, you're right. Let's go." She unbuckled, popped her door open, and hopped down onto the street. Devin jogged from the driver side of the truck to the sidewalk. They walked toward the intersection ahead. Caroline looked for their next path to take.

"Do you have a picture of her on your phone?" Devin questioned.

"Of course." Caroline fumbled to pull her phone from her pocket. She flipped the screen on and thumbed to a photo of Hayley, "See?"

"Perfect. We can show people the picture and find out if they've seen her at all."

"Good plan. Let's try the grocery store up there." She pointed across the street, "There's bound to be plenty of people in there."

"Sounds good to me." He said, "Let's hit it." The two of them ran across the street once an opening in traffic appeared. The sky grew darker as the storm clouds approached. The afternoon heat began to drop. Midday shadows had all but disappeared from the cloud cover. The glass store doors slid open and Devin ran inside, Caroline right on his heels. Several people milled about the store picking foods and fresh produce from the displays. Their calm demeanor was a stark contrast to the concern and panic of Hayley's sister. Caroline immediately jumped to the customer service desk to their right.

"Excuse me," Caroline frantically called out to the worker, "have you seen this girl?"

The worker looked at the photograph of Hayley and began to shake her head, "No, I'm sorry. I haven't."

"Okay." Caroline dropped her hands from the desk and turned back to Devin to deliver the bad news. Before she could even speak he grabbed her arm and pulled her toward the other customers.

"Let's keep moving, we can't stop now." He demanded. They approached each person they saw and showed them the picture of Hayley. Person after person, Aisle after aisle they searched yet could find nothing to help them in their search. Not a single person had seen Hayley. Caroline became increasingly frustrated each time someone was unable to help. Devin, however, only grew more determined to find someone or something that would help in their search. Nothing would stop him until they reached a final resolution to their ordeal.

Back to the streets they went. Chasing down anyone they could and seeking any information available. Each person they came across had the same answer. No. Not one single person had seen Hayley anywhere. They stopped to take a break from searching for a few minutes and to try to make a more thorough plan. They took a seat on a bench outside of the pharmacy. Caroline wanted to give up and stop searching, but she knew that she may never see her sister again if they gave up now.

The late-afternoon clouds continued to darken. They appeared as if they could open at any moment and soak the entire city. Caroline looked to the sky, she watched the dark clouds briskly float nearer across the horizon. The light gray bodies were being overtaken by darker and heavier cloud coverage. Trees began to curl and twist from the winds blowing away from the incoming storm. Caroline felt the wind from the nearby storm cooling her skin. The summer humidity had begun to break. Faint rumbles of thunder could be heard in the far distance. It would be upon them in no time.

"Devin, we've got to get going again," Caroline pointed out, "it looks like it's going to storm really soon."

"We have to keep searching, though, four hours is nothing." He said.

"I know," she admitted, standing and sticking her phone back into her pocket, "but we have to at least get back to your car so we can find more people. There won't be many people out anymore after the storm starts. Plus, it is going to get dark soon."

"I hear ya. Let's get going." Devin tapped his hand a few times on the armrest of the bench before standing up. He stretched his neck, arched his back, and let out a small groan. Caroline took the lead on the walk back to the truck. Devin followed right behind. They quickly walked the several blocks back to the car before they got caught in the rain.

= *26* =

7:30 P.M. The sun was starting to set behind the dark storm clouds. A light drizzle of rain began to cover the streets. Caroline and Devin continued to canvas the streets of Eden Isle in search of Hayley. The incoming rainstorm was sure to make the search much more difficult. "This is impossible," Caroline whined, "how are we supposed to find her in storm?"

"Don't give up, we're going to find her," Devin continued, "No matter what."

Caroline sighed and nodded. The distant thunder was nearly on top of them now. Flashes of lightning peppered across the sky, illuminating the streets like a mid-afternoon sun, providing brief moments of clarity. Caroline pulled her phone out of her pocket and called her mother.

"Hey Caroline." Amy answered.

"Hi, Mom," Caroline replied, "any luck yet?"

"No," Amy paused, "Not a thing. You?"

Caroline slapped her thigh in frustration, "No, we haven't gotten any farther either."

"That's what I was afraid of. Keep looking, sweetheart. I've got to go."

"Okay, Mom. I'll keep you posted." Caroline hung up the phone and turned to Devin. "My mom hasn't found anything yet either."

"Yeah, it didn't really sound too good when you were talking there." He tapped his thumb on the steering wheel, constantly looking back and forth across the streets for Hayley. Caroline impatiently bounced her foot on the floor of the truck. The rain continued to increase in its intensity. The dwindling daylight made the alleys nearly impossible to see into. Only small lamps above doorways within them provided any discernible visions of what lay beneath. The rain drops fell from the soaked street lamps and signage all around them. Pinging and tapping loudly off of the windshield and metal body of Devin's truck. Headlights shined across the roadways, reflecting off of the rain soaked streets and sidewalks. Night grew ever closer and darker. Visibility dropped more and more by the minute. Water splashed off the roads from the passing cars and onto the windshield. Caroline's demeanor began to drop as their search seemed to grow more hopeless with night approaching.

A large lightning bolt flashed across the sky. Caroline's head jerked forward as Devin slammed on the brakes. The truck slid to a rough stop, the rear of the truck spun slightly to the side. "Oh my God." Devin whispered.

"What are you doing?" Caroline questioned.

"I thought I just saw someone on the roof up there," he pointed to the apartment building straight ahead of them.

"I can't see anything up--" Another brilliant flash of lightning streaked across the late evening sky. The mysterious silhouette of a person shown against the lightning lit sky. The unknown person was nearly still atop the building's ledge. "Wait, I see someone up there too," Caroline added, "it couldn't be though, right?"

"Only one way to find out." Devin confidently quipped. He stepped firmly on the gas and accelerated toward the apartment building. The truck's tires spun on the drenched street before gaining traction and propelling the car forward. Cars parked on the side of the road whipped past the windows. Rain pelted the windshield of the speeding truck. Devin forcefully stomped the brake and pulled his truck to the curb. Caroline jumped out of the truck and onto the sidewalk. She looked toward the rooftop of the five story building shielding her eyes from the rain. The sky glowed again with a gleam of lightning. The figure was revealed once again, its hair blowing in the wind.

Devin jumped up to the curb next to Caroline and looked to the roof with her. The truck's engine remained running. Its headlights shined a glowing cone of light ahead. He glanced to the lobby and grabbed Caroline's shoulder. "You go inside and tell anyone that could help that there's someone on the roof."

"Okay, what are you going to do?" She asked.

He paused as if to deliver alarming news. "I'm going to go up there," he said as he pointed toward the roof, "I've got to see if that's Hayley up there."

Caroline's eyes opened wide, "Be careful," she pleaded.

"I will." Devin promised before darting to the side of the building.

Caroline ran through the front door of the apartment building. She searched the small lobby for anyone that could help. "Hello?" She called out, "Is anyone here?"

A small clatter came from a closet toward the back of the lobby. A few seconds later the old janitor poked his head out into the room, "Yes? Need something?" He asked. His gray facial scruff peeked out over his deep tan skin. The janitor stepped out of his closet and into the lobby.

"Someone is on your roof." Caroline sharply piped.

The janitor's ash eyebrows curled inward toward his nose, "What?" He questioned.

"They look like they're right on the edge, like they might jump." Caroline nervously added.

"Oh dear God, I'll go get some help." He barked and grabbed his keys from the hook in the closet. He ran from the lobby to the stairs, the door slamming behind him.

Caroline turned and sprinted back outside.

Devin climbed the fire escape along the side of the building. He ran the metal stairs, skipping one stair with each step. He gripped the handrail tightly with each bounding step. His foot slipped on one of the wet steps and he grunted in pain as he slammed his knee into the next stair. Regaining his balance he continued to run toward the roof. Thunder rolled along the skyline as lightning blitzed through the clouds overhead. The rain steadily poured from above and soaked his clothes. Floor by floor he marched to the top. His thighs burned from exertion. The fresh scrape and bruise on his knee stung with the edge of his shorts constantly rubbing against it. He continued to soldier on.

Devin grabbed the top of the fire escape tightly and pulled himself over the ledge onto the roof. The wind blew the rain directly into his face. He peered across the rooftop, the silhouette of the person, a girl, remained still, her hands lifted off of her sides. Devin was certain Hayley stood across from him. Her highlighted hair gave her identity away. Street lights below shined against the building and a small light above the door to the roof lit the area near where Devin stood. Thunder blasted overhead, the storm was right on top of them now. The strong winds tossed the girl's hair wildly. Devin cautiously snuck across the roof, "Hayley?" he announced. The girl did not acknowledge his call. "Hayley? It's me, Devin."

The girl slowly turned around to face Devin. Hayley. The small roof light softly hit Hayley's features. Her face deathly white and weak with exhaustion. She stood with her head tilted slightly downward. The bags under her eyes were deeper and darker than they had ever been. Dark streams fell from the corner of her eyes. The crimson rivers streaked to her jaw and dripped to the hospital gown she was still wearing. Rain soaked the gown and spread the blood across her shoulders and chest. The red pool soaked down to her stomach. Devin inched closer to her, "Hayley," he called out again louder to compensate for the noise of the rain and wind, "Hayley, can you hear me?"

Hayley stood motionless except for her mouth. She mouthed and mumbled incoherently. Her hands began to twitch and her head jolted back and forth. The shaking, as well as her breathing, grew more intense. She stepped backwards toward the ledge. Her bare foot stepping up onto the concrete sill of the roof. Devin took a deep breath, the rain continuously pounding his face. He walked closer and stretched his arms innocently out to his sides. "Hayley," he addressed, "please answer me."

Hayley's only answer came in the form of an inhuman grunt and growl. She lifted her head and stared directly back into Devin's eyes. Her eyes, completely devoid of color, were opaque black orbs. She turned her back on Devin and inched closer to the edge. "Hayley!" Devin shouted.

"No." Hayley snarled in a deep, raspy and tortured voice.

"Don't go any farther, Hayley." He commanded.

Behind Devin the sound of rapid footsteps climbing the fire escape were faintly audible. Caroline pulled herself up onto the rooftop and took several bounding steps toward Devin. He held his hand up to tell her to stop. She slowed to a halt and stood about a yard behind him. "Hayley," she whispered to herself, "I'm here."

Devin stepped closer to Hayley. He stood only a few steps from her now. She hunched over on the edge of the building. Her hands tightly clasped at her waist. Hoarse guttural growls escaped from her lungs. Devin reached his hand toward her, "Hayley, please come away from the edge."

Hayley growled and shook her head fiercely. She slipped her foot to the very edge of the roof, her toes gripping the concrete rim. "She's going to jump!" Caroline cried. Her tears hidden by the rain that drenched her face.

Devin waved his hand to quiet Caroline, "Hayley, don't do it." His words fell on deaf ears as Hayley appeared to prepare to launch herself off of the roof. Devin rushed to her side to grab her off the ledge. Hayley spun and lashed out at his face. Her nails sliced his cheek, leaving four cuts across his face. Devin stepped back grimacing in pain. He shook off the wound and jumped back to the edge. He lunged at Hayley and tightly wrapped his arms around her. Her feet slipping from the sill as he latched on. He used all of his strength to rip her from the side of the building. Devin fell on his back onto the rooftop. He held Hayley as tightly as he could manage, pinning her arms to her side. She thrashed and kicked violently in his arms. Devin pinned her to the ground with all of his weight.

"Caroline," he called out, "go get the truck."

"Right." she answered. Caroline ran back to the fire escape and back to the street. She jumped down the flights of stairs on the fire escape. The black metal frame creaked under her hard steps. Large drops of rain gathered on the underside of the escape and fell on to Caroline's head and shoulders. Her heavy, rain soaked clothes clung tightly to her skin. She hopped down from the fire escape to the alleyway below and sprinted back to the truck. Jumping into the driver's seat she shifted into drive and slammed her foot on the gas pedal. The truck jerked forward toward the alley.

Devin cradled Hayley over his shoulder as he carried her to the fire escape. She kicked her legs aggressively and thrashed her upper body. Devin locked his fingers together to keep her pinned to his shoulder. He slowly walked down the black steel staircase to the ground. His shoulders ached while trying to stabilize Hayley and keep his balance on the slick surface. Floor by floor his breathing grew heavier. His legs burned severely as he finally reached the pavement below. Caroline anxiously waited for them next to the truck. She ran to the back of the truck and dropped the tailgate.

Devin dropped his shoulder to lower Hayley into the truck bed. She clawed and scraped at him as he lay her down. He climbed into the truck bed with her to hold her down. Devin looked to Caroline, "You're going to have to drive. I've got to stay back here."

"Okay." Caroline said as she turned to climb back into the car. The rain had evolved into a torrential downpour. Thunder shook the night all around them.

"We've got to go get help. She's burning up. Her whole body feels like it's on fire." Devin called out from the back through the open rear window.

Caroline looked forward in determination, "I know where we have to go."

= *27* =

Rain pelted the windshield creating a blinding wall of water. The wipers whipped back and forth as fast as they could yet only created small bits of clarity before being nearly blinded again. Caroline sped through the Eden Isle streets. Devin held on tight in the truck bed while trying to keep Hayley under control. He opened the side hatch and pulled out two bungee cords and tied them around Hayley's wrists to keep her from clawing at his face. He hooked them onto the metal loops on the side of the truck. Rain dripped from every part of his face. A deafening crack of thunder crashed across the sky. As if the blast was a final buzzer the heavy rains broke and began to slow. Devin breathed a sigh of relief at the lightening weather.

Devin sat against the side of the truck bed. His arms and legs burned from exertion and he struggled to regain his breath.

Caroline sped and whipped the truck around the turns of the city streets. Its tires skimmed dangerously across the soaked pavement. Hayley struggled with the cords wrapped around her arms. She groaned and growled as she pulled fiercely at her restraints and kicked her feet into the sides of the bed.

Streetlights shined off of the road and wet cars lining the streets. The now calmly falling rain slapped the windshield of the truck as it accelerated onto the highway. Caroline aggressively drove in between the other cars on the road. Other drivers honked their horns at her because of her dangerous driving. Her nerves raced through her body. In her short time of having her driver's license, she had never been forced to drive like this before.

Caroline floored the gas pedal and the engine of the pickup truck roared. Devin held tightly onto the edges of the bed. The rain continued to fall at a slow but steady rate. Due to the wind from the speed of the truck, the rain felt like needles to his skin. He ducked behind the cab of the truck to avoid the stinging drops. The small back window in the center of the cab provided a solid handle to grip along with the passenger side of the truck bed.

Devin braced himself against the side and grabbed the cord holding Hayley's wrist to pull himself up to a crouched position. Caroline pulled the truck up behind a slow moving car. "Come on, move!" she shouted. She started to switch lanes and accelerate. The red car ahead of her also attempted to move over. "Oh my god!" Caroline yelped as she jerked the wheel to the left to swerve around the car. Devin lost his footing and fell into the side of the truck. His back bent over the top edge and caused him to nearly fall out onto the highway. He cried out in fear. Headlights shined through the front window of the truck as a car horn blared ahead. Caroline swerved back into her lane and Devin fell onto Hayley in the bed of the truck.

Hayley attempted to lurch out at Devin. The bungee cords pulled taught as she tried to extend her hands around his neck. She fought the tight straps and stretched them as far as her muscles could manage. She snapped her jaws towards his head. He pulled himself back up against the front of the bed, his heart racing. "Sorry, Devin," Caroline called out from the front, "I'm trying my best."

"It's alright. Just try to be careful from now on." He wiped the rain away from his face and ran his fingers back through his hair. Slouching back down on his bottom he massaged the tender new bruise on his back. The rain began to intensify again. "Oh great," Devin quietly said to himself, "just what I needed." He glanced up toward the sky. The storm continued on its path over the area. Lightning streaked from cloud to cloud, lighting up the skies.

Eden Isle faded away in the darkness behind them. The highway extended over the waters of Lake Pontchartrain. Darkness spread in every direction as far as the eye could see. Devin stared out into the dark abyss around him. The lightning sparked and flashed in the distance as thunder rumbled throughout the night skies. Rain danced across the surface of the lake. The expansive night surrounding them made the drive feel as if it would never end, that they would never get the help that they needed.

Caroline stepped on the gas again hoping to shave any number of seconds she could off their travel time. She planned to head straight back to the Jackson Square area and retrace her group's path through the neighborhoods as she could not recall the exact location of Astrid's shop. She hoped in the back of her mind that the shop was still open. The highway soon gave way for the bayous on the outskirts of New Orleans. Devin tapped his hand on the back of Caroline's seat, "So where exactly are we going?"

Caroline quickly glanced over her shoulder at him, "It's really hard to explain. It's near Jackson Square." She turned her head back toward the road, "I just think that it's what we need to do."

"Whatever you think will help." Devin looked back to Hayley. Her face had all but lost the last remaining bit of color it held. The blood seeping from her eyes had been mostly washed away from her cheeks by the rain. It left light streaks in all directions across her skin. Each drop of rain that hit the stains pulled some of the bloody tears along.

"We're getting close to the Square." Caroline called. Hayley thrashed about in the truck bed. She kicked her legs again and again, loudly growling and moaning. Her kicks began to get slower. She tried to tear at the straps on her arms again before her body gave out and she fell motionless in the bed.

"Hayley?" Devin asked. He looked down at her seemingly lifeless body. Her pale skin was lit by the tail light above the cab. Her blackened eyes appeared a deep amber in the red light. "Hayley?" Devin asked again and tapped her cheek. She remained deathly still.

"What's going on?" Caroline asked.

"Wherever we're going you better step on it, kid," Devin frantically said, "She's not looking too good."

Caroline punched her foot on the gas. The truck sped through the bayou park on the edge of New Orleans. Trees flashed past the windows of the truck. The foliage lightly covering the sides of the road peeked through the heavy shadows. Wind shook the truck roughly on the road. Leaves and small branches whipped across the pavement and smacked into the truck's windshield.

The lights of New Orleans appeared in the distance as the bayou disappeared behind them. Small lights shone from the windows of homes and businesses along the highway. "How far away are we?" Devin asked.

"Only like ten minutes," Caroline answered, "I'm going as fast as I can." The truck sped through the streets of New Orleans, Jackson Square neared ever closer.

"Okay," Devin said placing his hand on Hayley's forehead, "She getting really cold back here." Devin reached his hand into the back of the truck cab and pulled out a large plaid blanket. He tossed the blanket over Hayley's body, "This will only help for a little bit until it gets too wet. Stay with us, Hayley."

Caroline's nerves worsened after hearing Devin talking to Hayley. She was terrified for her sister. Terrified at the thought of losing her.

= 28 =

Caroline slammed on the brakes and the truck skidded to a stop halfway onto the sidewalk outside of the Hallows of Mystery entrance. Its back end remained sticking out in the street. The roads surrounding the shop were populated by a few empty cars and random bits of trash in the gutters. The late night summer thunderstorm raged outside as the black pickup truck pulled up to the old store. Devin looked around the car, confused at their final destination. "What the hell are we doing at a bookstore?" He barked.

"This is where we need to be," Caroline turned off the truck's engine, "I told you it's hard to explain, but there was a woman I met here that seemed to know way too much about what was going on."

"What? How would she know that?" He asked.

"I don't know," She answered, "but I think we're about to find out. I just hope she's still here."

Devin jumped over the side of the truck bed and down to the street, leaving Hayley tied in the back. "Let's go find out."

Caroline popped out of the driver's seat and jogged around to meet Devin in front of the truck. Rain continued to pelt the pavement around them. The rickety sign above the door swung and creaked in the heavy wind. She walked to the door and pulled the handle. Locked. She pounded on the glass windows of the door, "Astrid!" she shouted, "Astrid, open the door!" There were no signs of motion or activity inside the store. The lights inside were off. Raindrops obscured the visibility of the store windows. Only small areas of the shelves could be seen through the dusty glass. Caroline slammed her fist into the door again. "Open the door!" Frustrated, she backed away from the door and looked around the storefront.

Devin firmly grabbed Caroline's shoulder, "Up there." He pointed his finger above the store. The glow of a small gas lantern shined through a cloudy second story window over them. A shadow partially blocked the light before moving away from the glass.

Caroline glanced to the window. "It's got to be her." She stepped back toward the truck and looked around for some way to get the attention of the person in the window. An empty crushed soda can sat on the ground near the back tire of the truck. She picked it up and took aim at the window. Caroline flung the can toward the window. It bounced off of the siding on the second story about two feet below the window. It deflected off of the roof and fell back to the ground in front of her. Devin grabbed it from her feet and threw it back at the window. The metal pinged solidly off of the center of the glass and came to rest on the roof. "Astrid!" Caroline screamed.

Devin gave three resounding pounds on the door. The sound echoed through the shop. The shadowy figure appeared in the window once more. Her bony hand slid the window open. "Who is out there?" Astrid asked in her raspy, smoky voice.

"It's Caroline. You kicked me out of your store yesterday."

Astrid's eyes narrowed as if she was looking at an enemy, "Why are you here? I told you to never return."

"We need your help," Caroline sighed, "I know that you know what's going on with my sister. It's time for you to fix it."

Astrid disappeared back into her room. "Where did she go?" Devin asked.

Caroline shook her head, "I don't know."

"What's her deal?" He inquired.

"She's mean. She snapped on me when we came in on our trip." Caroline pointed to the store's front window, "We came in and we got talking about Hayley and she seemed to know way too much about it. So I kept asking her about it and she just went off and kicked me out."

Astrid turned out the lamp and the room went dark. Caroline placed her ear against the damp glass of the front door. The store was silent. Only the sound of the falling rain could be heard. She impatiently tapped her fingers on the door while she tried to hear any commotion inside. Her light taps grew firmer and more frustrated the longer she waited. Caroline lowered her head off of the glass, she sighed and stepped away. "No, no, no, no," she vented. Her frustrations boiled over as she stomped back to the door. Caroline bashed her hand against the glass once more, "Astrid! I know you're in there!" she shouted.

Devin placed his hand on her back between her shoulders, "Come on," he whispered, "we have to figure something else out."

The tears in Caroline's eyes were hidden by the rain running down her face. She looked to Devin, hoping to see some hope in his eyes. He gave her a small half smile and lightly guided her toward the truck. Caroline took a couple steps before Devin grabbed her arm again. "Wait," he chirped, "look."

A lamp in the back of the shop was lit and Astrid slowly crept out of the back room of the shop. She cautiously guided her fragile body across the shop floor toward the front door. Caroline darted back to the door and awaited Astrid's arrival. Her nerves gave way to an overwhelming sense of determination to get some concrete answers about her sister's condition.

Astrid's bony hand gripped the lock and slipped the chain out of the track. The tarnished gold doorknob jiggled as she gripped and twisted it. A weathered slow creak rang out as she pulled the door open. Her dark gray eyes peered through the small gap between the door and frame. "What do you want?" Astrid grumbled in a dark hoarse tone.

"It's my sister," Caroline's voice shook as she held back her tears, her seemingly ever present emotional state now, "she's getting worse. I think you're the only one that knows how to help."

"I knew you would be back," Astrid smirked, "the evil always comes full circle."

"What is that supposed to mean?" Devin hollered from behind Caroline.

Astrid opened the door and signaled to Caroline, "Come. Bring her inside." A loud thunder clap shook the buildings and echoed down the street.

Devin ran back to the truck and climbed into the bed. The rain pelted the hard lining in the back of the truck. He removed the bungee cords from the hook and untied them from Hayley's wrists. The water from the truck bed dripped from the open tail gate to the ground below. Devin pulled Hayley to the edge and lifted her limp body on to his shoulder. He balanced her waist atop his shoulder and carefully walked back into the shop.

Caroline was toward the back of the shop when Devin returned from the car. She brushed her hair with her hand and squeezed out any water she could. Shuffling footsteps could be heard coming from the second story above. "She said she's going to get ready," Caroline explained, "she told me to stay here."

"Has she given you any information yet?" Devin asked.

"No, but we're not leaving until she does."

"Good idea," he added, "this needs to end now."

Astrid's feet clopped down the wooden stairs back into her shop. "It is ready."

"What's ready?" Caroline inquired.

"Come upstairs."

"Tell me. Right now," Caroline demanded.

"The ritual," Astrid confessed.

= 29 =

Caroline and Devin carried Hayley's battered body into the mysterious second story of the shop, both visibly shaken and extremely nervous. A lone window was directly in front of them. The same gas lantern that shined to the street sat on the window sill. An old worn arm chair sat next to the window. Candles were placed in several places across the empty floor. Piles of boxes lined the wall to their right. Astrid awaited their arrival in the center of the room. She sat on the floor surrounded by the pale candles, mirrors, and tattered old books. Chalk lines and large circles were drawn on the floor. Caroline recognized this quincunx Astrid had made. This makeshift Hoodoo crossroads would likely serve as the centerpiece to this ritual. Fear quickly devoured any composure that Caroline and Devin could muster.

Astrid looked up from her seat and met both Caroline and Devin's eyes with an unnerving stare. Her eyes appeared almost blood red in the glow from the candles. There was a certain unexplainable glassiness to them, appearing almost lifeless. A foreboding energy enveloped the room. Like something out of a horror movie, the thunder and lightning had become the score for the ritual. Astrid rose from her statuesque seated position.

"Place her in the center of the crossroads, only she can decide where she is to go from here." Astrid instructed in her scratchy voice. "We will need to restrain her so she stays within the circle for the duration of the ritual." Devin firmly placed his hands on Hayley's shoulders and Caroline pinned her legs to the floor. Her legs began to twitch and flex again in the center of the crossroads. Chalk smeared on the wooden floor and stained the back of her heels. Her upper body followed suit and began to convulse.

"Very well," whispered Astrid, "soon the spirit will be mine."

Caroline perked her head up, "What? Why would you want to keep the spirit here?"

"That is not for you to know." Astrid firmly snapped.

"No. It *is* for me to know. This is my sister we're talking about here."

Astrid sat across the quincunx from Caroline. "You know not the true power of what you are dealing with."

"Tell me." Caroline gritted through her teeth.

"The spirit within her is stronger than you know. The controller of the spirit is able to manipulate minds for their bidding. Trapping the spirit in a stone prevents this from happening."

"So get this thing out of my sister so it can't hurt her anymore." Caroline commanded.

Astrid calmly dropped down to her knees and placed a book and large gemstone in front of herself. She turned her palms toward the floor and moved them in large circles over the stone and book. "Arise spirit within," she spoke in a deep monotone voice, "You are summoned from your host."

Hayley sharply jolted on the floor as if she was being called to attention. Her chest lifted off of the wooden planks. Her shoulders and legs remained pinned by Devin and Caroline. A deep growl started in her chest and made its way up to her throat. Astrid continued to perform her ritual, her words turning from English to an unknown language.

"What are you doing to her?" Devin fiercely questioned.

"She must be brought into the battle. The evil cannot be defeated by ritual alone. I must take the demon from her."

"Why do you have to take it?" He asked, "Can't you just trap it again?"

"Silence, boy. You do not understand what you are toying with. You are in danger here." Astrid's warning struck a chord in Devin's mind and he rose to his feet.

"In danger of what? Why do you want the spirit so bad?" He growled, looking down to Astrid.

"You do not need-"

"Answer me!" He shouted and kicked the book away from her hands, "If you don't we will take her away from here and find someone else who can help us." Devin leaned down to lift Hayley from the ground.

"Wait." Astrid sighed, "Be warned, your anger will dig your own grave one day. This girl is a powerful vessel. She holds within her a spirit that has killed many others who have been cursed. I chose her for this very reason."

"You *chose* her?" Caroline chimed in confusion.

"Yes. She has become my vessel to return my spirit to me. Ash has dwelled within me for ages. I have cursed my chosen victims to do my own bidding, until now. Like a wild horse, the spirit of the victim must be broken. She proved to be my strongest victim. A will power so strong that it could not be shattered. The distance between myself and the accursed weakens my hold upon them. Now that you have brought her to me, I can finish my work. With her spirit combined in the stone, my power will be endless."

Caroline paused and her brow furrowed, "What are you?"

"Long ago, A shaman burned down my home and killed my family. I was driven away from my homeland, but I have sought revenge for it ever since. She is the most powerful vessel I have found. Many have died from the curse. She is the chosen one." Astrid lifted her head slightly. Her eyes fixed upon Hayley.

"Chosen one for what?" Asked Caroline.

"She is mine to exact my revenge upon he who cursed me." Astrid muttered.

Devin shook his head, his anger boiling over, "She's not yours to take."

Astrid's eyes had drifted away from their natural gray tones and turned an opaque white, as if cataracts had completely taken over. "I take who I want." Her normal raspy voice had been replaced by a deep and demonic tone. She thrust her hand out toward Devin. A powerful force emanated from her body and tossed Devin across the room like a ragdoll. He slammed into boxes at the far end of the room and crashed to the floor. The impact left him motionless on the hard floor.

"Devin!" Caroline cried out. Her voice was a mixture of shock and worry. She turned to Astrid and angrily asked, "What is the matter with you?"

Astrid ignored Caroline's question. She pulled the book and gemstone that Devin kicked back in front of herself. She scribbled down a short passage on the page with a charcoal pencil. Caroline leaned over to see what it said but Astrid's handwriting was too shaky to read.

Astrid lowered her head to the floor, placing her hands ahead of her shoulders. She began to mumble incoherently toward the floor. Slowly her head rose and her gaze pointed directly at Hayley, whose body now lay rigid on the floor. With two strong open palm slaps on the floor, chalk dust blew into the air. Astrid leaned back and placed her weight onto her heels. She raised her hands out to her sides and tilted her head back and faced the ceiling. "Sah cor fou ra laer," she called out. Caroline wiped her tears away at the sound of the strange language. Her vision remained blurry as Astrid continued. "Vash tou coule yahfet lah." Astrid began to shake her arms and a deep hoarse moan escaped her throat.

Caroline's nerves twisted her stomach into knots at the bizarre sight. Hayley's body began to convulse and lift off the floor. Her body rose completely off the crossroads and levitated nearly two feet off of the floor. Dark growls and moans manifested and intensified in Hayley's chest. Her unconscious body turned in the air and rolled into a fetal position facing the floor.

Astrid lifted the book and gem off of the floor. "Ash, I call out to you!" She shouted. "You are me, and I am you. Return to me, flame of vengeance, and reignite the fire within."

Hayley lifted her head and opened her eyes. Ash had taken control of her body. Tears of blood seeped from her blackened eyes and rolled down her cheeks, staining the floor and chalk lines below. Her head twitched and turned. "Silence!" The room echoed with Ash's deathly response. "You are nothing."

Astrid's book floated off of her hands and into the air. The passage on the page began to release and turn to black smoke. Small sparks jumped from the spine of the book and ignited the dry pages. The book erupted into flames in mid-air. Astrid raised her arms toward the ceiling and the fire exploded outward, shattering the window behind them. Hayley's convulsing began to worsen. She was at war within herself. The deep growls were now being interrupted by small bursts of Hayley's true voice. Her youthful sound tore through the beast's power over her body. She pulled and ripped at her hospital gown. The chalk below her swirled in the air from the wind coming through the broken window.

Hayley's breathing grew very deep. Each breath longer than the last. Her entire body tensed as she took one final deep breath. "Get Out!" Hayley released the command in a long blood curdling scream. Flames burst from her body, missing Caroline's head by inches. She ducked to the floor and covered her eyes. Astrid was knocked to the floor by the force of the blast. The remaining glass of the window was blown out into the streets. The gemstone on the floor exploded into dozens of deep green shards.

Fire swirled around the room. Hayley's gown caught fire and the flames instantly engulfed her body yet she remained unharmed by them. The flames began to spin and turned straight to Astrid. She became encircled by the spiraling tower of flames. Embers from the fires filled the air. Astrid gasped and flames forced themselves into her lungs. Her eyes began to glow a bright orange. The flames were burning her from the inside out. Her skin cracked and dried and split. Flames broke through the rifts across her body.

The roaring fire began to burn away Astrid's clothing and hair. Her painful screams did nothing to stop her own destruction. Soon the flames began to destroy the very fabric of her body, burning her flesh away, turning her bones into dust, and reducing her entire body to a pile of ashes. The swirling wind scattered Astrid's ashes across the floor. Astrid, the deceiver, had been killed. Destroyed by her own evil greed.

Hayley fell hard back down to the floor. A room that just seconds ago was filled with an inferno, was now completely still. Caroline lifted her head at the newfound silence. She looked back to the crossroads. The chalk that lined the floor had been completely blown away. Hayley's body sat motionless on the floor. "Hayley?" Caroline whispered. Hayley slowly moved her hand to her stomach. She let out a quiet pained moan.

The boxes that Devin crashed through shifted and he cautiously propped himself back up to a knee. "What in the world just happened?" He asked in between coughs.

"She's dead." Caroline answered, astonishment in her voice.

"Hayley's dead?"

"No," She cracked a smile, "Astrid."

Devin looked around the room for Astrid's lifeless body, "How?"

"I- I don't know. Everything was on fire and then it all stopped."

Devin got to his feet and shuffled to Hayley's side. He knelt by her side and grabbed her shoulder. "Hayley, are you there?"

Hayley moaned and turned her head toward the sound of his voice. She coughed dust and ashes out of her lungs, "Devin?" She weakly said while wiping the blood from her eyes.

"Yeah, it's me. Caroline is here too."

Caroline's eyes opened wide at the sound of Hayley's voice. "Oh my God!" She exclaimed, "I thought I would never see the real you again."

Devin hugged Hayley close. He placed a light kiss on her forehead. Caroline's eyes welled with tears as she wrapped her arms around her sister. "I'm so glad to see you, Hay."

"What happened? Where are we?" Hayley asked. She gingerly placed her hand upon the floor and pushed herself up. She rose from the ashes, determination burning in her veins.

Caroline brushed dirt and soot from her clothing and started to explain the whole ordeal, "New Orleans. You were being taken over by-"

"Stop." Hayley cut her off, "You can tell me later," she squinted harshly and placed her hand on her temple. Just get me home. Just get me home."

Through the flames, a life tempered and turned.

Lessons unchained from the pages burned.

No matter how strong your demons may seem,

Your heart is always stronger.

- FIGHT -